INSTINCT
FOR
SURVIVAL

SAUL WARSHAW

Cover Design by Lee Helton

Full Moon Publishing, LLC
Glade Spring, VA
Fullmoonpublishingllc.com

FULL MOON
PUBLISHING, LLC

ISBN: 1946232491
ISBN-13: 978-1946232496

CONTENTS

ACKNOWLEDGMENTS

If you're a major league baseball fan, you no doubt have heard about Shohei Ohtani, the Los Angeles Angels multi-talented pitcher and hitter – the first player to handle both roles, in some 50 years.

Well, I've been blessed with a similar, multi-talented person. His name is Rob Stock. And he has been of incredible help in my writing of Instinct for Survival, as well as the multi-book Will Jonas Mystery series.

First reader, grammarian, proofreader, story line suggester, general encourager, good friend – these are the talents that Rob applies, for my benefit.

Thank you, Rob!

Saul Warshaw

CHAPTER ONE

The Year: 1964

"Ever hear of a man named Jacob Kaufman?" The questioner was Chief Immigration Service Officer William Craig, head of the New York office. He was talking to Mike Taylor, a special investigator for the Service.

Mike shook his head. "I don't think so. It's a pretty common name, though. Must be a lot of them around."

"Yes, but there's only one we're interested in." Craig looked at his watch. "And you've got an appointment with him in an hour and a half."

"What's the problem?" Mike asked with increased interest. It wasn't like Craig to play things so tightly, leaving only an hour or so for a complete briefing session on a new case. Obviously, Jacob Kaufman, and whatever problems he brought, had come into being only a short time ago. It was probably about the time Craig had called last night.

All Craig had said then, was, "Be at my office at 9:00 sharp, tomorrow morning."

Mike had been working out of the New York office for more than two years, but he and Craig were not on a first name basis. Craig was a leathery old bastard, and not the kind to get too friendly with his staff.

Although most of the men in the office were somewhat awed by Craig's rough manner, Mike wasn't. And he was quick to question Craig when he had called.

"What's up?" Mike had asked. "I was going over to the court house in the morning."

"Nothing I want to discuss on the telephone. Except to tell you that you can plan on dropping everything else, and taking on a special assignment. Something where your concentration camp and war crimes experience will come in handy. Be here at 9:00." Craig had hung up, leaving Mike with a dead telephone and a lot of questions.

Now, in Craig's office, the latter started to answer Mike's questions.

"What's up is a lot of problems," Craig said, tapping the thick manila folder that lay on his desk. "Enough problems for the State Department to be interested, and for a few choice directions from the White House, too." He looked intently at Mike. "What goes on from this point, Taylor, is strictly confidential," he warned. "The only person to whom you will make reports from now on, is me.

Everything written, everything said, comes right to me. Marked, for my eyes only. Understood?"

"Yes," Mike answered, more puzzled than ever. What the hell was Craig leading up to?

Last night, after Craig had hung up, Mike had tried to figure it out. Craig's mention of the concentration camps and war crimes could mean any one of a dozen different assignments.

True, the Nuremberg Trials had ended 18 years ago, but periodically, individual Nazi fugitives had been found, arrested and tried. Adolph Eichmann as recently as 1962, when Israel's Mossad had captured him in Argentina and brought him back to Israel for trial. He'd been found guilty and was hanged.

Mike shook his head. Here it was, 1964, and there probably were still some war criminal fugitives out there. Would it ever end?

Unconsciously, Mike's mouth had become set in a grim line. No, he answered his own question. It should not end. Not until every last war criminal was made to pay!

Then he had relaxed. Still the same old story, he had thought with amusement. Mention the camps, the war crimes, the poor, miserable displaced persons, and he was frothing at the mouth again.

It had, in fact, been this same intense anger that had led him into the Immigration Service after World War II. During the war, Captain Mike Taylor had carved out a well-deserved reputation for himself in the Army, first as an undercover liaison man with resistance groups behind the lines in Italy and France, and then as an investigator with the Army War Crimes Commission in Germany.

He was a lawyer by training, though he hadn't had a chance to practice, having enlisted in the summer of 1941, right after graduating from law school.

Mike had applied a lawyer's careful logic to his Army undercover work. The result was an efficient and effective liaison man who had been air dropped into Italy and France nine times during the war, to make contact with the partisan groups.

Though Mike had never been wounded in any of his undercover work, he had one indelible memory of it. His hair had turned completely white. It presented an arresting contrast to the rest of his appearance. He was tall, about 6 feet 2 inches, and athletically built. A rigid adherence to exercise had kept him in shape, despite his age, which was 43. His slightly lined face was on the dark complexioned side, and its somewhat stern outlook was softened by his eyes, which were brown and wide set. The nose was long and straight, and flared slightly at the nostrils.

Right after the war had ended, and before he had been mustered out, Mike had been assigned by the Army to do investigative work in connection with the Nazi war crimes trials that were then being planned. And although he had grown accustomed to cruelty and brutality while dealing with the partisan groups, it was during his investigative work with the War Crimes Commission that he really began to feel the human race had hit bottom.

In his work, Mike had to visit the concentration camps. Auschwitz, Belsen, Dachau, Buchenwald and the others.

He had seen and spoken with the poor miserable remains of human beings, mostly Jews, who had survived the horrors. And it had made a deep impression on him.

When Mike had finished his War Crimes assignment, to return to civilian life, the prestige offers rolled in from several New York law firms. His fine academic record, combined with his war hero role and crimes commission work, were enough to insure an excellent job.

But to the consternation of his friends, and delight of his new wife, Claire, Mike had turned aside all the offers, and had accepted a civil service appointment with the Immigration Service.

Claire. The thought of her brought back the pain. The pain of seeing her crumpled body in front of the car.

It was because of Claire, that he had found it easy to reject the lucrative offers and accept the relatively low paying job with Immigration.

Claire had said to him, "Since I am a new immigrant myself, Michael, how can I not feel that your work with the Immigration Service is the most important thing?"

This had been her only comment, when Mike had asked her if she minded the fact that he was rejecting jobs which offered much more money.

Idealistic? Yes, he knew that. But it was how he felt. He

believed that by entering the Immigration Service, he could help some of those sad displaced people he had seen at the end of war.

He went to work as a special investigator for the Immigration Service, concentrating on clearance checks of potential immigrants. His duties were similar to police investigating, though rarely dangerous.

Claire and he had been intensely happy in those first years. And then she had been killed when a car struck her, outside their apartment in Washington.

That was 11 years ago. And since then, Mike had remained unmarried. For most of the time, he had been assigned to various cities, the latest of these being New York. Here, his work had been routine enough up to now. But Mike sensed this was going to change, as he listened to Craig explain who Jacob Kaufman was.

"Now, about Jacob Kaufman," Craig began, "Although his name's not very well known, Jacob Kaufman is an extremely successful, and important businessman here in New York. He's in the import-export business, dealing mainly in art items. Paintings, antiques, sculpture, stuff like that. But what is important is his political background." Craig leaned forward. "It seems that Jacob Kaufman is on a first name basis with just about every important national political figure in the country. And that means right up to the White House. He's been a very big political contributor for years. But his connections aren't only because of the money he spends. Kaufman is supposed to be one of the top advisors to the New York state and national Democratic parties."

"A guy, with eminent connections," Mike interjected.

Craig nodded in agreement. "But for our purposes, here's the most important point. Kaufman is a survivor of Dachau. One of the few Jews to get out of there alive. What's more, his wife and daughter are survivors of Auschwitz."

So here's where I come in, Mike thought, as Craig continued speaking.

"Two days ago," Craig said, consulting the manila file folder, "Jacob Kaufman received the fourth in a series of threatening letters. Letters from someone who says he is going to kill Kaufman and his family. The letters aren't signed, of course, and about the only identification we can figure out is a phrase the writer keeps using to describe himself as," Craig glanced down at the open file and quoted from it, "'a good German who knows he must kill you to save the world from Jewish financial and political domination.'"

Mike felt the anger well up in his throat, while at the same time, he experienced a sense of compassion for Kaufman and his family. To have survived the horrors of Dachau and Auschwitz, and now to have this hit them. "Some bastard nut," he said harshly.

"Maybe," Craig allowed. "In fact, probably, But there's a complication. And it's what is worrying the State Department, and the White House."

Craig got up and began pacing about his office. "I don't know how closely you follow foreign policy matters, Taylor, but I guess you're aware enough to know that DeGaulle can at times be one big pain to our State Department and its NATO defense planning."

"Yes. I'm aware of that."

"Well, as a result of DeGaulle's independent policies, there's a growing feeling in the State Department, and elsewhere in Washington, that France can't really be depended on, in the eventually of some kind of ground war in Europe."

"That's some pretty sweeping kind of thinking," Mike observed. "I find it a little hard to believe, myself."

"That's neither here nor there," Craig answered. "I'm just giving you the background as it is. Our personal opinions don't count for very much in all this," he said impatiently.

"Sorry," Mike said, thinking that he had never seen Craig so agitated. Whatever the problem was, it seemed very clear that the pipeline extended right up to the top in Washington.

"The theory," Craig continued, "is that if France can't be depended on, then more reliance must be placed on Germany. And naturally, if this is to be the case, then Germany must be strengthened militarily. More men in uniform, more arms, and, the eventual possibility of atomic bombs under German control."

"Brother," Mike said, shaking his head, "is that one going to be hard to sell the people."

"Precisely," Craig agreed. "And let's not even think now about whether it's right, wrong, or what. No matter whatever you or I feel, the fact remains that this is a growing line of thinking among certain factions in Washington."

"I still don't see how Kaufman fits into all this." Mike said.

"Remember when the first German troops were organized in the late 1950's? Or when the first Germans went into maneuvers in France? Or when some German soldiers came over here, for advanced training a few years ago? Remember what happened?"

Mike nodded. "There were plenty of demonstrations. Everywhere."

"Correct. Along with a lot of comments about how could we rearm the German beasts, etcetera, and etcetera."

"Rightly so, as far as I'm concerned," Mike said strongly, despite Craig's earlier warning about letting personal feelings interfere.

But this time, Craig didn't seem to notice. "Well, think about this for a minute," he said. "Here our State Department is, dickering with the idea that perhaps, just perhaps it might be of value to start rearming Germany. The Department knows there will be a tremendous, negative public reaction to this thinking. But, it is conceivable, the Department reasons, that if things are explained logically enough, the nation's, and the world's sentiments, can be brought into line. After all, Germany has been on such good behavior for so long now, they're our staunch allies, and so on. Make sense? At least as a possibility that the State Department should consider?"

"All right. I'll go along as far as that," Mike conceded. "I mean, I realize we've got to consider all the alternatives. And there is some feasibility to this one."

"That's exactly what their reasoning is in Washington," Craig went on. "But now, we come to Kaufman and the threatening letters he's been receiving." Craig stopped his pacing and stood over Mike. "Just what the hell do you think would be the reactions of people, if, on the one hand they were being asked to have faith in the new Germany, while on the other hand, it was learned that threats were being made on the lives of three persons who had survived Dachau and Auschwitz? Three people who managed to escape the wholesale slaughter that killed six million other Jews?"

"The State Department could most definitely forget about even thinking of re-arming Germany for another 100 years," Mike replied. "There'd be pressure, not only here in the U.S., but probably from around the world."

"Right. And mind you, I said only if it was learned that threats were being made on Kaufman and his family. How much worse would it be if they were actually killed."

"Worse for whom? The Kaufman's or the State Department?" Mike asked icily. Try as he could, he was unable to divorce his personal feelings from the problem!

Craig looked sharply at him, then nodded in understanding. "I know it sounds harsh to speak of this only in political terms, rather than talking about the lives of three human beings who've suffered more than enough, already. And I'm aware of why it hits you especially hard. But we've got to."

Then he said, "I'm assigning you to find out who's been writing these threatening letters to Kaufman."

"Me? Isn't it kind of an unusual assignment for someone in

Immigration? More the kind of thing the CIA or FBI would be doing, I would imagine."

"Usually, yes," Craig answered, "but there are good reasons for it being you. First, you've got a perfect cover story. You're going around, asking questions about former immigrants like Kaufman and his family, is completely natural – in line with your present work.

Second, no one would suspect an investigator for the Immigration Service of being involved in anything so political as this, something that involves foreign policy and the like. A State Department investigator? An FBI man? Someone from CIA? They'd all be suspect. You're not."

"Who do I work with?" Mike asked.

"No one. You're going to be on this investigation alone. And you've got carte blanche on where you go, what you do, who you see. It's all yours."

"Isn't that kind of odd, on something as big as this?"

"The thinking is, the fewer people involved, the less the chance of anything getting out. After all, it may all just be a crackpot writing letters to Kaufman, and no one in Washington wants to dignify this by any large scale investigation. That might really botch things up, if the information leaked."

"Anything I find out, I report to you? Not the State Department, or anywhere else?"

"Right. Even though State has ordered this investigation, the Department won't even acknowledge that you exist. Absolutely no trace must ever be established between the Kaufman case and the State Department," Craig warned.

"You say I've got carte blanche," Mike went on, wanting to establish clearly in his mind the exact procedures under which he would be operating, "but does that mean up to, and including the actual arrest of the would-be assassin?"

"No, it doesn't," Craig answered. "I was about to explain that to you. What you have to do, is find out who is behind this. Once that's established, the decision will be made in Washington as to what happens next." Craig raised a warning finger which he used to punctuate his next remarks. "Under no circumstances, except an extremely unusual emergency, are you to make the final arrest. You just find out who it is. It'll be handled by other people after that. Is that completely and clearly understood?"

"Yes," Mike said.

"Good." Craig handed the manila file folder to Mike. "You have an appointment with Kaufman at 10:30 in his office. You'll find all the details in this file, including copies of the four threatening letters. Kaufman will be expecting you."

"You aren't coming?" Mike asked.

Craig shook his head. "As of right now, you are on your own."

CHAPTER TWO

Kaufman's office was uptown, on 57th Street, between Park and Madison, an area where there were several art galleries. Mike decided to take a cab, from his office at the Federal Building at 120 Broadway. It would enable him to look through the file on Kaufman, and give some thought to the case.

For a while, as the cab sped up the East River Drive, Mike studied the file. But now, he closed it, and looked blankly out the window, toward the East River. He took a deep breath, hoping it would ease the tension that was building in his stomach.

It was always the same, whenever he became involved with anything relating to the horrors of the German concentration camps. He grew both sick with disgust and tense with anger.

These two feelings had been his strongest in those first weeks after the war, when he had led an investigating team into Belsen, Auschwitz, and finally, Dachau.

Dachau. That was where he had met Claire. She was an inmate, and had been brought into his office for interviewing.

Claire Vadim, her card had read. She was French, an

underground resistance fighter, who had been sent to Dachau for extermination in the Summer of 1944. But because she wasn't Jewish, and because the all-devouring goal of the Dachau authorities had been to kill as many Jews as possible, the death of Claire Vadim had not been hurried.

Her attractiveness, too, had something to do with it. "I still had a good figure, then, a useful figure," she told Mike, her voice devoid of feeling, when he naively asked how she had been able to survive.

Clumsily, he apologized for his stupid questioning. She shrugged. "It does not matter now. Nothing can be changed. The dirt of it is too deep."

The dirt of it is too deep. The way she said the words, so dully, and yet so full of desperation. At that moment, all of the compassion that had been building up in Mike over the past weeks, as he had visited the other camps, rose to meet Claire's words. Perhaps because she sensed this, Claire responded to Mike. And that had been the beginning of a relationship that only the violence of the car accident had been able to end.

Because, through Claire, Mike had learned so intimately of the horrors of the concentration camps, his pity now went out to Kaufman. To have lived through so much, he thought to himself. And now, to face this stupid threat from the past.

"You want me to make the turn onto 57th or let you off at the corner?"

The cabbie's question brought Mike back to the present. He

told the driver to let him off at the corner of 57th and Park. A few moments later, Mike reached Kaufman's office. The small, dignified lettering on the hall door read, "Jacob Kaufman. Import & Export."

Mike opened the door and walked into a large reception room, which was tastefully furnished in Traditional. A receptionist took his name and relayed the information inside. Shortly, a middle aged, gray haired woman came out and asked him to follow her.

Mike accompanied the woman down a corridor, to an oak paneled door. Once there, the woman knocked on the door, then opened it and stepped aside, motioning for Mike to enter. He walked past her into the room, and heard the door click softly behind him.

"Mr. Taylor." The voice, low and well-modulated, had traces of a German accent. Its owner was of medium height, with dark brown hair that was thinning on top and graying on the sides. He was dressed impeccably, the fine tailoring helping to hide the beginnings of a pot belly. That Jacob Kaufman was now living well, after his wartime horrors, was obvious.

"I am glad that you were able to come so quickly, Mr. Taylor. I am Jacob Kaufman."

Mike shook Kaufman's outstretched hand. "I'm happy to meet you, Mr. Kaufman. And I hope I can be of service to you."

Kaufman smiled gratefully as he led Mike to a couch near one end of the office. He picked up the conversation.

"And I also hope you can be of service to me. And to us," he added, nodding toward a double picture frame on the table in front of the couch. There were portraits of two women in the frame, one middle aged, the other appearing to be in her twenties.

"Your wife and daughter?" Mike asked.

"Yes. And the main reason why all of this troubles me so much." Kaufman picked up the picture frame and handed it to Mike. "You see my daughter, Mr. Taylor? Do you not think the photographer has caught a quality of... of tranquility...of peace...in her expression?"

"Yes. It's a lovely picture," Mike answered.

Kaufman smiled. "Excuse me. Of course you would not be in a position to judge what expression of Ruth's is tranquil, or what in her face seems peaceful. You do not know her." Kaufman's face grew hard, as he looked intently at his daughter's picture. "I, however, can judge, Mr. Taylor. And this picture, taken only last month, is a peaceful Ruth, a happy Ruth."

He put the picture back on the table and turned to Mike. "For many years, since the end of the war, Ruth's moments of peace and tranquility were only fragmentary. They were merely short periods, occurring between the depths of depression and her withdrawal from reality. Do you understand what I mean, Mr. Taylor?"

"There was something in the file about your daughter having...uh...having had to spend some time under psychiatric treatment."

Kaufman sighed. "You say it delicately, and with diplomacy. Thank you. But we must speak frankly. It is a fact that Ruth spent three years in a private sanitarium, under intense care." He looked tenderly at the picture of his daughter. "But two years ago, she effected a full recovery. And last year, she met a man and fell in love." Kaufman looked across at Mike. "They are to be married shortly, Mr. Taylor. And it is for their sake…and especially for Ruth's…that these letters trouble me so much." Kaufman leaned toward Mike. "I must impress this fact upon you, Mr. Taylor. I am greatly afraid of how Ruth would be affected, if she were to find out about these threats. And furthermore, I do not have any intention of ever letting her know. She must have her opportunity now for happiness. She must!"

"You believe that if Ruth found out about the threatening letters, it might set her back again?" Mike asked.

Kaufman nodded. "It was her original experiences as a small child at Auschwitz, that led to her mental upset. And this reopening of old wounds…" for emphasis, Kaufman hit his knee with his fist…"my daughter must never know of this matter, Mr. Taylor," he warned. "I would rather die a thousand times by burning, than have my daughter learn any of this. The consequences to her would be too dreadful to even contemplate!"

Mike thought for a moment. "How about your wife? Does she know anything about this?"

"No. And I do not want her to know, either."

"It may be necessary, however, at some point," Mike cautioned. "As we get into this, there might be something your wife can tell us that will help. So I hope you won't' consider it an impossibility that I may have to speak with her."

"Let us try to avoid it as long as possible?"

Mike nodded in assent. "Agreed."

"Thank you, Mr. Taylor. And now, how can I help you? What can I tell you?"

Mike took out the case file and opened it. "I've examined the threatening letters, of course. There are only these four? You haven't received any others?"

"No. That last one arrived 6 days ago. And that was when I requested help of the State Department."

Mike shuffled the letters in his hand. "Milan, Paris, Florence and Rome. In that order. The letters came from those cities, over a 9 week period?"

"Yes."

"Do you know many people in those cities?"

"Of course. Quite a few. I have business dealings in all of them."

"Can you think of any enemies you might have in those cities? Possibly persons who might feel you've gotten the better of them in a transaction. For example, have you made any art purchases in those cities, and then realized a big profit on the deal?"

"What you are asking is, if someone might have cause to be angry because I bought something from them, and subsequently sold it at a much higher price?"

"Exactly. I know this is a real possibility when dealing with paintings. Is there anyone you can think of, who might be disgruntled about this?"

Kaufman rubbed his hand slowly across his mouth, hesitantly. "Mr. Taylor...you...you understand that I...I do not wish to cause an innocent person any trouble...by...by accusing that person unjustly..."

"Do you have someone specific in mind?" Mike asked quickly.

"Well, it is only a very, shall we say, a very weak and probably totally unjustified suspicion..."

"Suppose you let me judge that," Mike interrupted. "Now... who is it, Mr. Kaufman?"

Before answering, Kaufman rose from the couch and walked slowly about the office, head lowered, his hands clasped behind his back. "Ever since the first of these letters arrived, I have of course been thinking. Thinking and attempting to determine who might be behind this. And just as you, my thoughts turned to my past business dealings." He paused. "One name does keep occurring to me, Mr. Taylor." He looked apprehensively at Mike. "But it is such an awful thing. To accuse a man of this. I do not like to do it..."

"Who is it? Mike demanded."

Kaufman hesitated again, but finally spoke. "His name is... Behrens. Otto Behrens."

"Behrens," Mike repeated. He looked at the letters. "Behrens. That's a German name, isn't it?" He asked, remembering

19

something Craig had said to him. He searched through each of the letters, his head nodding in confirmation as he found what he sought. "Look," he indicated to Kaufman, "there's one phrase that appears in all four of these letters. Here it is. Where the writer describes himself as, 'a good German who knows he must kill you to save the world from Jewish financial and political domination.'"

Kaufman asked, "Do you think since Behrens is German, this phrase might connect him with the letters?"

"Well, didn't you have the same thought?" Mike pointed out.

Kaufman nodded. "Yes...I...I did."

Kaufman raised his hands in despair. "Mr. Taylor. I do not like what I am doing. God knows, I have no love for Germans, or for Otto Behrens. But, I...these accusations I am making. I am deeply disturbed by them. I am acting no better than the Nazis did..."

"Mr. Kaufman." Mike interrupted. "I appreciate your feelings. And I can only assure you that Otto Behrens won't be judged unfairly by us. Please. You must believe that."

Kaufman sighed, then nodded. "All right, Mr. Taylor."

"Now," Mike put the letters back in the file and took out his note pad, "tell me all you can about Behrens. And about your business dealings with him."

"There is not very much to tell," Kaufman answered, as he returned to the couch. "I have not seen Otto Behrens in five years. And although we had some art transactions which were highly profitable to me, I feel I gave him a fair price for his services."

"Did he ever seem angry about your dealings with him? And the profits you made?"

Kaufman opened and closed his hands thoughtfully. "Mr. Taylor. Again, I...I do not feel right about the accusations I may be making. You see, Behrens was angry with me. That is true. But he is a naturally excitable person. Sometimes, he even imagines certain slights." Then he added quickly, "but this far...to go this far...well...it is hard to believe of Behrens."

"You say you haven't seen him in five years," Mike persisted. "Do you know where he is now? Where he lives?"

"Probably in Rome," Kaufman answered. "He has lived there since the war. He used to have a small office near the Piazza di Spagna, on Via di Babuino, number 82, I recall. It may still be there. But in any event, I would imagine the Rome Art Dealers Association would be able to tell you where he is now located."

Mike took down the address Kaufman had given him. "Was Behrens a Nazi in Germany during the war?" he asked. "And do you know why he hasn't gone back to Germany to live?"

Kaufman shook his head. "I do not know the answer to either of those questions. Was he a Nazi? I do not know. After the war, no German was a Nazi," he said bitterly. "Nor do I know why he has not been living in Germany."

"All right, let's leave Behrens for now," Mike continued. "He's only one possibility, and a thin one at best, anyhow. So let's look into some other alternatives. For instance, if we assume these letters are from some ex-Nazi, because of that anti-Semitic phrase,

21

then do you have any idea who it might be? Even the slightest suspicion of anyone?"

"No. I have thought and thought, Mr. Taylor. And all of my thinking results in nothing."

"How about when you were in Dachau? Would there be any of the guards who, for some reason, might have remembered you?"

No...no. I was only one of the thousands. One of the faceless victims. I am sure there was nothing I did which made me stand apart." Kaufman smiled thinly. "The instinct for survival, Mr. Taylor. It makes one try to be as inconspicuous as possible. And not to stand apart."

"Well, then, how about some of the Germans you knew before the war?" Mike consulted the file. "Some of the people you knew in Berlin? You lived there all of your life, didn't you?"

"Existed, would be a more accurate way to describe it," Kaufman said with bitterness. He shook his head. "No. I have also thought of that possibility, Mr. Taylor. And other than the continuing misery inflicted upon us by almost everyone, there was no person in particular who would have reason to remember me now. And besides, that part of Berlin where I was born and lived, it is now in East Berlin. Even if there were anyone, how could that person possibly have the freedom to travel to all the cities from where the letters were mailed?"

"Good point," Mike conceded. "But please. Let's think about it once more, Mr. Kaufman. You see, we've got a problem here. Normally, I'd want to go back in your history, and check the

22

Germans with whom you might have come in contact before the war. It's impossible to really do this, of course, because of the East Berlin situation. So that makes it all the more important for you to think about it as carefully as possible. Now. Are you sure there's no one from that part of your life, the part from before the war, who might be behind this?"

Again, Kaufman shook his head. "I can think of no one."

"All right, then let's try something else," Mike said. "Could the letter writer be someone from your wife's or your daughter's past? Any enemies they might have had?"

"I do not think so. Of course, Mr. Taylor, you are aware that I met my present wife, and Ruth, after the war?"

"Yes. I read about it in the files."

"She and little Ruth were as I was," Kaufman said softly, almost to himself. "Homeless. Each of our families murdered. Our lives seemingly destroyed." He smiled. "And yet, we have been able to rebuild." He turned to Mike. "And this cannot be destroyed now, Mr. Taylor! It must be prevented. At all cost!"

"I understand your anxiety, Mr. Kaufman," Mike assured him. "We'll do everything in our power to get to the bottom of this."

"I am certain of that, Mr. Taylor. Please," he said apologetically, "you must excuse me if I become excited..."

"Of course," Mike said quickly. "I know how much this must hurt. It was that way with Claire, too."

"Excuse me? Claire?"

"My wife," Mike explained. "She also was in Dachau."

Kaufman was obviously startled by this information, and his knuckles turned nearly white as he tightly grasped his knees.

Mike spoke again, quickly. "I'm sorry. I didn't mean to disturb you. I didn't realize the coincidence would trouble you so much."

"How could the State Department do such a stupid thing!" Kaufman said harshly. "Assign a man to this case who has a wife from Dachau. Obviously, you will talk to her about this case. And that is bad! It must all be kept secret! Secret, I tell you!"

Mike was surprised at Kaufman's continued agitation. And he also was angered at the other man's lack of confidence in his ability to keep the investigation secret. But the anger lasted only a few seconds, as Mike realized how great a strain Kaufman must be under. He sought to reassure the other man.

"Please, Mr. Kaufman. It's all right, I tell you. Nothing to worry about. You see, Claire is...is dead."

"Dead?"

Mike nodded. "She was killed in a car accident, 11 years ago." Kaufman appeared to calm down somewhat, and then he spoke.

"I...I am ashamed of myself, Mr. Taylor. To have said what I did."

He looked at Mike.

"Can you forgive me for my boorishness? It... it is only because of my present anxiety about these letters..."

"Of course," Mike assured him. He closed the file and put his note pad away, preparatory to leaving.

"What will be your next step, Mr. Taylor?" Kaufman asked.

"Go to Europe. Start with Rome, since that's the last city from which a letter was sent. And then, depending on what develops, go to the other cities, also."

"I see," Kaufman said. He paused, and then seemed to make up his mind. "Mr. Taylor. You have been so understanding, that I hope you will forgive a final, and I am sure, unnecessary plea for caution. My daughter. Her happiness is of the utmost importance to me. She must know nothing of this. You will be cautious, Mr. Taylor? Please?"

"Don't worry, Mr. Kaufman. I am sure we'll clear it up. Probably some crackpot. And you just happen to be the unfortunate victim of what I'm sure are his perfectly harmless letters."

"Hopefully, you are right," Kaufman said. He rose and stretched his hand out to Mike. "Thank you, Mr. Taylor. And God speed."

They shook hands and Mike turned and walked to the door.

As he did, Kaufman asked him a final question. "Mr. Taylor…do you carry a gun?"

Mike nodded. "Yes, Mr. Kaufman. I do."

CHAPTER THREE

Mike returned to his seat as the 707 jet started to swing into its landing pattern for Rome. He looked at his watch. Still a good half hour before they arrived at Fiumicino Airport.

He felt only moderately tired from the 9 hour flight. The shave he had just taken had refreshed him somewhat, and now he was looking forward to showering in his hotel. Then, he'd be ready to begin.

Begin where? By visiting Otto Behrens' last known office address, he had already decided. Via di Babuino, number 82. Not that he was planning to talk the Behrens. He didn't want to do that. Not yet. It would be too ticklish. After all, Behrens' involvement at this point was an extremely circumstantial supposition. Just some reluctant thoughts on the part of Jacob Kaufman.

However, Behrens was the only real suspect Mike had at that moment, so he had decided to start with the German. And the first thing he wanted to find out was, Behrens' traveling schedule, if any, in recent months. Had he been in Rome, Milan, Florence or Paris on dates that coincided with the postmarks on the letters received by Jacob Kaufman? If so, then Behrens could be moved up, to become a more important suspect.

Mike also wanted to find out if Behrens had any typewriters in his office. If he did, then were any of the four letters Kaufman received, typed on the machines in Behrens' office? That would certainly be a positive clue.

Of course, Mike cautioned himself, he had better not get too set on proving Behrens' involvement, at the expense of other possibilities. Yes. There were many other leads he'd have to check out.

For one thing, he wanted to talk to several art dealers in Rome, and find out what they knew about Jacob Kaufman and his business dealings. Perhaps one of them would be able to tell Mike about a disgruntled dealer who held a grudge against Kaufman, someone that even Kaufman didn't suspect. It was entirely possible, in the creative and emotion-charged world of art. The letter writer could even be an obscure painter whom Kaufman might have slighted or snubbed at some point.

And Mike also wanted to visit the Dachau concentration camp, near Munich. This would be to run down another lead, the possibility that one of the former camp guards or officers had somehow singled out Kaufman, and was now behind the letter writing.

Of course, Kaufman had been sure there were no Germans at Dachau who would have picked him out. But, after all, Mike reasoned to himself, Kaufman was a very successful man now.

And perhaps one of the Germans from Dachau now remembered him, and was resentful of his success. That certainly would fit the behavior pattern of an anti-Semitic and bitter ex-Nazi.

Mike's further theorizing was interrupted by the steward's voice on the intercom, requesting that the passengers fasten their seat belts. Well, Mike thought as he strapped himself in, I should be seeing a lot of Europe in the next few weeks.

About four hours later, Mike left his Rome hotel on the Via Bocca di Leone and began walking toward the Piazza di Spagna, which was only a few blocks away. He decided to walk up the narrow Via Condotti, one of Rome's most fashionable shopping streets, which led directly into the Piazza.

Mike knew Rome fairly well. In addition to having spent several months in the city during the war, he and Claire had visited it twice in the early years of their marriage.

He reached the Piazza di Spagna and looked across at the Spanish Steps. At their top, the cross of the Chiesa della Trinita dei Monti, the Church of the Trinita Dei Monti, caught the late afternoon sunlight. There were the usual tourists scampering about the Steps, many of them snapping pictures, the rest just looking. And at the bottom of the Steps, the same flower stall Mike had seen on previous visits.

He allowed himself a brief moment to look at the beauty of the Piazza. Then he turned to his left and walked toward the nearby Via di Babuino, the street which contained most of Rome's art and antique dealers.

As Mike threaded his way through the heavy crowds on the side walk leading out of the Piazza, a short, thin man began moving in the same direction. The man took care to keep at least a half block in back of Mike. He was dressed neatly, if inconspicuously, in a gray suit of a decidedly European cut, the lapels rather wide, the jacket somewhat fitted. He would easily have been indistinguishable in any crowd, were it not for a slight limp in his left leg and the scar on the lobe of his right ear. The scar was a deep red, where a poor suturing job had been done to repair a jagged tear.

As the crowd lessened on the Via di Babuino, the man dropped back to about three quarters of a block behind Mike. Occasionally, too, he glanced at the store displays, seemingly appearing to be window shopping. Then, when he saw Mike stop before number 82, the man quickly stepped into a store doorway.

Mike, unaware that he was being observed, stood in front of number 82 and looked at the name plates bordering the entrance. There was no plate for an Otto Behrens. He decided to go inside. Perhaps there was a more complete directory in the hall, or someone around who could answer his questions.

He didn't locate any directory inside, but he did find an elderly man, who seemed to be in charge.

"Parla inglese?" Mike asked. If pushed hard, Mike could carry on a halting conversation in Italian, thanks to his wartime duty. But in a situation like this, when he wanted to be certain of his facts, he preferred to speak English if possible. Luckily, the man spoke

English, of a broken variety, but understandable.

"Si," he reassured Mike. "I am able to speak English."

"Are you in charge of this building?"

"Pardon me?"

"Do you…do you take care of this building?"

"Oh. Yes. Si. Yes, I am in charge."

"Well, I'm looking for someone. But I don't see his name on the directory. Perhaps you can help me?"

"Si."

"His name is Behrens. I was told he had an office here."

"Signor Behrens?"

"Yes. Otto Behrens. He is an art dealer. Do you know him?"

"Si. Signor Behrens had an office here. On piano number 2."

"The second floor? Well, isn't he here anymore?"

"No. He closed his office,"

"When was that?'

"Perhaps two months ago."

"Did he move out entirely? Is there anything left up there?"

"Nothing." The man shrugged. "There was only a little furniture. And this he sold. There was nothing left."

"Well, did he leave any address? Any place he could be reached?"

"No." The man shook his head. "He merely came to me one morning, he handed me the key, and he said he would no longer need the office." Again, the man shook his head. "It was early in the month, also, and the rent already paid. But Signor Behrens said he did not care."

"Didn't care?"

"About the rent he had already paid. It was all so strange."

"Why was it strange?"

"Well, Signor Behrens, never did he smile. And it seemed as if he always wore the same suit. But that morning. He…he was very happy. And smiling. And he was wearing a new suit. A very nice looking suit. And smiling so. It was strange, I tell you."

"Has he ever come back again?"

"No,"

"While he had his office here, did he have many visitors?"

"No."

Deciding there was nothing more to be learned, Mike took the 100 lire note that he had been keeping in his hand, and passed it over to the old man. "Grazie," he told him.

"Prego," the man answered as Mike turned and walked to the exit.

As he reached the street, Mike considered what his next step should be. Behrens was no longer at the only address he had for him, and the trail was about two months old. He decided to visit the Rome Art Dealers Association. Perhaps they'd have some information as to Behrens' whereabouts.

Mike started walking in the direction of the Association's office, still unaware that the small man in the gray suit was again following him.

CHAPTER FOUR

"Behrens? Otto Behrens?"

"That's right," Mike assured Signor Veranti, the Director of the Rome Art Dealers Association. They were seated in the latter's office. After showing his Immigration Service credentials, Mike had quickly been ushered in, and had just finished explaining to Signor Veranti that he was doing investigative work, and that he wanted some information on Behrens.

Signor Veranti pushed a buzzer on his desk, and when his secretary came into the room, he directed her to check the membership files for a card on Otto Behrens.

While they were waiting for the secretary to return, Mike began questioning Signor Veranti. "Do you know Behrens?" He asked.

"Not well. But I am familiar with him."

"How long has he been in Rome?"

"Since the end of the war, it seems to me."

"Is he much of a factor in the art world, here? I mean, is he an important dealer?"

"No. Not very important." The Director thought for a moment. "In fact, you might say he hardly counts. He has only handled an occasional important transaction. More of a hanger-on type."

"I just came from the building where he used to have his office. He moved out about two months ago, I was told. Have you seen him in Rome since then?"

"Yes, I have," the Director answered. Then he added, thoughtfully, "More often than I used to, in fact. Now that I think about it, he seems to be at many more of the openings, the showings. Odd. Quite odd."

"Why is that odd?"

"Well, for one thing, he seems…better dressed. Yes. Definitely better dressed. And he is far less sour, too. That always was one of his problems. Like many Germans, he took himself far too seriously, and for absolutely no good reason."

The Director's secretary returned and handed him a file card. The Director looked at it. "Otto Behrens? Business address, Via di Babuino, number 82?" he asked Mike.

"That's the one."

Signor Veranti looked at both sides of the card. "Well, there is no other business address given on here. And you say he is no longer at number 82."

"I just came from there. Tell me, is there any home address for him on that card?"

"Yes. The Albergo Dante. Do you know the place? It is on the Via Principe Amedeo, near the railroad station. A rather shabby second class hotel."

Mike took out his note pad and wrote down the address. Then he asked, "What does Otto Behrens look like? Or better still, would you have a picture of him in your files?" Kaufman had already given Mike a description of Behrens. But that had been a product of Kaufman's five year old memories, and Mike wanted to check its accuracy.

"No, we do not have pictures of our members," Signore Veranti answered him, "so I cannot aid you in that manner. But of course, I can describe Behrens. He is slightly shorter than I am. I believe that would make him approximately 5 feet and 9 inches. He must weigh... about...155 or 165 pounds. He has a broken nose. It is not flattened. Rather, it is bent to the left side of his face. Not badly so. But enough to be noticed. Is that helpful to you?"

Mike nodded. The description tallied with Kaufman's. He rose to leave. "You've been very helpful," Mike assured Signor Veranti. "And, of course, your...uh...your discretion in this matter would certainly be appreciated by my government?" Mike hoped the Director would understand his unspoken request that their meeting be kept quiet.

"Of course, Mr. Taylor," the Director assured him, as he shook Mike's hand and ushered him out of the office.

CHAPTER FIVE

The small man in the gray suit turned and looked into the store window. He watched as Mike came out of the Association's building, walked to a nearby taxi stand and climbed into one of the vehicles. Then, as Mike's taxi started to pull away, the man hurried to another cab and told the driver to follow.

Up ahead, Mike thought about what he would do, once he arrived at the Albergo Dante. He decided he couldn't just barge in and ask too many questions about Behrens. No telling how close the concierge and Behrens might be. So, he would need a good reason for asking questions. That was obvious.

But what should that reason be, he asked himself. For the next several minutes, as the taxi sped toward the Via Principe Amedeo, he examined a number of possibilities.

"Albergo Dante, Signore," the driver announced a short while later, as he veered his taxi to the curb.

Mike checked the meter, added an extra 150 lire to the 850 that showed, and gave the driver two 500 lire coins.

The Albergo Dante, as Mike turned to face it, definitely looked second class. Probably toward the bottom of the class, at that, Mike thought, as he entered the small lobby and looked for the concierge's post.

The lobby was empty, and the man behind the concierge's desk looked up with only minimum interest as Mike approached. As soon as he recognized Mike as an American, however, he managed a professional smile.

"Buon giorno, Signore," he said, standing up. "Can I help you," he added in English.

"Perhaps you can," Mike said. On purpose, he kept his voice low and confidential. He leaned over the concierge's desk and a 5000 lire note appeared next to the concierge's hand. A quick, practiced movement of the hand, and the note disappeared.

Thank god for the Latin love of bribery, Mike thought to himself, as his 5,000 lire offering was rewarded with a now very friendly smile from the obviously interested concierge.

"It is rather a...a delicate matter," Mike continued, his voice still low. "A...shall we say...a thing of the heart..."

This second calculated appeal of Mike's, this time to the Latin romantic temperament, had its desired effect. The concierge leaned forward expectantly, now seemingly a willing participant in whatever it was that Mike wanted to discuss.

"What is it I can do for you?" he asked Mike.

"I come here at the request of a friend of mine," Mike told him. "An American, living in New York." Mike looked around the lobby and then stage whispered, "You see, this man, my friend, has reason to believe that his wife has been having an affair with someone who lives in Rome."

"Ah," sighed the concierge with full understanding.

"And my friend has asked me to learn all I could about this person in Rome. The one he suspects. But of course, we do not wish to arouse his suspicions."

"Of course," the concierge agreed. He cleared his throat, and then he bit at the bait, just as Mike had hoped he would. "This, uh, this person. You believe he lives here? At the Albergo Dante?"

Mike nodded. "Yes. And I would like to ask you some questions about him. Without his knowing about it, of course...?"

"Of course. Of course," the concierge agreed. "Who is it? Who is this man?"

"My friend thinks it is a...a Signor Otto Behrens..."

The concierge stared at Mike. He seemed puzzled and unbelieving. Then he shrugged. "Anything is possible, of course. But Signor Behrens? Who would have thought it? In all these years..."

"You know him?" Mike said quickly, seeing an opportunity to start asking direct questions.

"Si."

"How many years has he lived here?"

"For at least five years." The concierge shook his head.

"But for him to have had an affair with this woman. With any woman at all..."

"Why do you say that?" Mike asked.

"Signor, he...he was like a...a pickle, this Behrens. Never a smile. Almost never a word. And a German, too," the concierge added with distaste.

"Did he seem to spend a lot of time here?" Mike asked, anxious to see if the concierge knew anything of Behrens' traveling habits, especially about any trips to Florence, Milan or Paris. "I mean, did he leave Rome often?" Again, Mike leaned close to the concierge. "My friend has reason to believe that his wife has been meeting this Behrens in other cities. Places like Florence, and Milan, and Paris..."

"Yes. Yes," the concierge exclaimed, now fully caught up in establishing this new and more interesting image for the previously dull Signore Behrens. "Those very cities are where Signor Behrens has traveled. And many times!"

Mike stood up straight and nodded his head. He almost had to suppress a smile as he continued to play his role with the anxious concierge. "I see," he intoned. "It is beginning to fit together, my friend. It is beginning to fit together." He pulled out his note pad and consulted it, looking for the dates of the postmarks on the letters that Kaufman had received from Milan, Florence and Paris. "Can you tell me when Signor Behrens last went to each of those cities?"

Mike waited tensely while the concierge thought about the question. Then, the Italian snapped his fingers, dove beneath the counter and rummaged around for something. A moment later, he came back up, with a beaten ledger book in his hands.

"At times, when he expected to be away from Rome for a considerable period, Signor Behrens had me forward his mail to him," the concierge explained to Mike as he quickly turned the pages. "Ah, yes. Here is the last time I sent him mail in Florence. It was on the 22nd of August."

In spite of himself, Mike almost gave a start. The date the Florence letter had been sent to Kaufman was August 24th. So, the two dates certainly were close enough together to make it entirely possible for Behrens to have sent the letter!

"And the hotel to which you forwarded the mail?" Mike asked.

The concierge checked the entry in his ledger. "The Albergo Aprile, Via Della Scala, number 27."

"And how about the dates and the hotels in Milan and Paris? Do you have those?"

"If Signor Behrens directed me to forward mail to him, then I have the information," the concierge said, looking through the ledger. "Yes. Here is Milan. The date for this was, July 14th. And it was the Albergo Tonale, at Via Pecchio, number 2. And," he paused as he sought the information on Paris, "in Paris, I sent mail on August the 1st, to the Montpensier, at 12 Rue de Richelieu."

Again the dates matched! Behrens had been in both Milan and Paris, at approximately the same times as the postmarked dates on the letters sent to Kaufman.

"The times are the right ones, eh Signore?" the concierge

asked, wrongly interpreting Mike's intense interest as being related to the supposed assignations of Behrens and the American lady. "Signor Behrens, the quiet one, has traveled much with his American lady?

"It would unfortunately appear this way," Mike said seriously, again playing his part. There was more information he wanted from the talkative concierge. But before he could resume his questioning, the other man spoke again.

"He was indeed a careful person, Signor Behrens," the concierge said, almost in admiration. "In all of the time of his living here, never once did he bring the woman...any woman...to the Albergo. In fact, there is only one time, in all the years, that anyone came here to see him. That time, it was two men. And it was a strange visit, too."

"Strange? How?" Mike asked cautiously. This was beginning to get a bit away from the romantic angle, but Mike thought it might be worth pursuing, just so long as he didn't arouse the concierge's suspicions. The latter, so thoroughly caught up in the intrigue of it all, was only too willing to let Mike in on all the details.

"This was not too long ago, Signore. In the late evening. At 10:00 or 11:00. First there was this little man. Nervous. With a limp. And with a red scar. Here." The concierge indicated the lobe of his right ear. "He asked if Signor Behrens was in, and he then went into the next room and spoke with him on the telephone. Then, when I went into the office," the concierge indicated the room directly behind him, "a second man came in, and the two of them took the elevator to see Signore Behrens."

"What did the second man look like?"

The concierge shrugged. "I could not see him well. His hat was worn low, he kept his collar up, and he walked very quickly. But it was obvious that he was rich. Yes. Very rich."

"Why do you say that?"

"Ah, I know clothes, Signore. Once, I used to work in a clothing store. And I know a fine suit when I see it. And an expensive hat. A very expensive, how do you call it, a homburg?"

Mike had another question he wanted to ask. His tone again grew confidential. "There is one more fact which has led my friend to believe that his wife is having an affair with this Behrens. It is the letters that she has received." Mike paused to give his next words added emphasis. "Love letters."

"Ah…" the concierge nodded understandingly. "Of course."

"These letters," Mike continued, "they have been typed. So, tell me, do you know if Signor Behrens has a typewriter?"

The concierge shook his head. "He does not have a typewriter. This I know for a fact. And how do I know it?"

"How indeed?" Mike fed him the question.

"Because Signor Behrens often would ask for the typewriter in the office to be sent up to his room," the concierge announced triumphantly. "The typewriter is for hire, in the evening, when the office is not in operation," he explained further.

"I see," Mike said, deliberately appearing to be thinking aloud.

"It may be the very typewriter on which Signore Behrens wrote his…his love letters to my friend's wife. We must find out. Signore, may I be allowed to type a moment on that machine?"

"Of course," the concierge said, taking Mike by the elbow and guiding him into the office. "It is yours to use, Signore."

Mike spotted a piece of blank paper and he put it into the typewriter. Then, with the concierge leaning anxiously over his shoulder, Mike carefully pecked out, mainly for the concierge's benefit, "My Dearest Alicia. The time we spend apart is an agony of existence for me. I cannot much longer endure the waiting until we are together again. We must meet soon."

Mike examined the type carefully. A number of the individual characters were distinctive enough in their style so that Mike was just about sure. Of course, he would have to check against the photostats of the Kaufman letters he was carrying in his suitcase. But he was almost certain that this typewriter had been the one to write the Rome letter that had been sent to Kaufman!

"Well, Signore? Is it the correct typewriter?"

The concierge's anxious inquiry reminded Mike of the role he was playing. Solemnly, he looked up at the concierge. "It is the correct typewriter."

"Mama mia," the concierge muttered. "Signore Behrens. It is so difficult to believe."

Now, Mike was anxious to leave the hotel and be rid of the concierge. But first, he wanted to make sure the other man kept his confidence and didn't reveal their meeting to Behrens.

"I have learned what I need to know," Mike assured the concierge as they returned to the desk in the lobby. "But of course," he said seriously, "It would not do for Signor Behrens to learn of our discovery. My friend in the United States would not want Signore Behrens to suspect anything. You understand, of course...?" Mike asked, as another 5,000 lire note found its way from Mike's hand to the concierge's.

The concierge beamed. "Of course, Signore. I understand completely. But there is really no need to worry. No need at all. For you see, Signore Behrens is no longer here."

"No longer here?"

"Si. He moved out. A few days after the two gentlemen visited him."

CHAPTER SIX

The next morning, in Frankfurt, the ringing of the telephone in his hotel room roused Mike from his sleep. He groped for the receiver, brought it to his ear, and heard the words, "Guten morgen. Good morning. It is 8:00."

"Danke schoen," he managed to slur out of his sleep locked mouth. Putting the receiver back on its cradle, Mike decided he could allow himself of a few more minutes in bed. He relaxed his body as he thought again about the reasons that had prompted yesterday's sudden decision to come to Frankfurt.

He had made the decision after learning that Behrens had written the letter on the rented typewriter at the Albergo Dante. Although this information was promising, Mike realized that in a situation as delicate as this investigation, such evidence certainly wasn't enough for any direct State Department action with the Italian government. A lot more would be needed.

His first impulse, then, had been to follow Behrens' trail to Florence, Milan and Paris, and establish whether Behrens had also used typewriters in each of those cities, to write his threatening letters to Kaufman.

But one point had nagged at Mike. None of this evidence would help to establish a motive for Behrens' actions. Why was he threatening Kaufman?

On this point, Mike had a feeling, and it was nothing more than that, he admitted to himself, that the answer could be found in Kaufman's past history. Possibly during the time he had been imprisoned at Dachau. Perhaps, Mike theorized, Behrens had been a guard there, even though Kaufman didn't remember him in that role.

So, Mike had decided to come to Frankfurt, where the German government had been holding the records of the war crime trials. The government's Frankfurt collection of documents and records, including those on Dachau, were about the most complete available, anywhere.

Mike wanted to look at the records. Spend no more than two or three days in satisfying this hunch of his. And then it would be back to Rome, to pick up Behrens' trail, or to one of the other cities. He didn't think he'd have any trouble actually locating Behrens. The man obviously wasn't hiding, if Signor Veranti of the Art Dealers Association had seen him at several functions in Rome recently.

Mike threw aside the covers and started to get out of bed. He had a 9:30 appointment with a Herr Meisner in the Frankfurt War Crimes section of the Federal Bureau of Records.

Promptly at 9:30, Mike was shown into Herr Meisner's office.

The latter was a tall and stout man who wore rimless glasses. He had only a few long strands of hair, fighting to cover his broad expanse of otherwise bare head, and he seemed to have a permanent slouch to his shoulders, as a result of being with records and catalogs for the major part of his life.

After greeting Mike, Herr Meisner smiled encouragingly at him. "Mr. Taylor, I have been requested by my government to be of service to you in every way possible. Now, how may I help you?"

Mike nodded. Evidently his boss, Craig, while voicing some doubts about the need for Mike's trip to Frankfurt, had nonetheless quickly and effectively cleared the way for him. They had spoken by transatlantic telephone late yesterday afternoon.

Mike returned Herr Meisner's smile. "I'm interested in doing some research into the concentration camp records," he explained. "Mostly on Dachau, for the present. Perhaps on some of the others after that."

"May I inquire if there is anything in particular for which you are looking?"

"At this point, it's a little uncertain. I'll probably have a better idea once I can find out what sort of cataloging arrangement you have here."

"Of course."

Herr Meisner leaned to the left of his desk and pushed a button. Then he addressed Mike again. "With your permission, I will turn you over, now, to my assistant, who will be able to inform you as to the cataloging, and offer any other services you may require."

Mike hardly had time to thank Herr Meisner, before a door opened at the far corner of the room, and a woman entered. Mike's first curious glance quickly turned into an interested look.

The woman was tall, perhaps five seven or eight. Age, 28 or so. Her figure was trim with hints of possibly interesting curves and lines allowed to show from beneath the business suite ensemble she was wearing. Her blond hair was cut slightly on the short side, and swept back quite simply.

But, it was the woman's face that commanded the most attention. In pure physical form, it was quite attractive in combining the Germanic traits of fresh-as-peaches complexion, the large blue eyes and the complimentary topping of blond hair. Its attractiveness was enhanced by a seriousness of manner which seemed to mould the facial features into a perfect form.

But rather than being attracted, Mike was slightly repelled. Not strongly and overtly. Rather, in some quiet way, which had nuances of a past time. And then, as the woman walked toward him, Mike realized the reason.

His intense dislike of Germans, smothered by someone like the scholarly Herr Meisner, who could have passed in any American college town as a typical professor, flowered in the presence of this woman, who was so typically Germanic in her appearance.

Recognizing, however, that he would have to work with the

woman, Mike tried to put his personal feeling into limbo, as he rose to meet her.

"Mister Taylor, may I present my assistant, Miss Herrman. Miss Herrman, this is Mr. Taylor, the United States government official whom I mentioned to you yesterday afternoon."

They shook hands, and then Miss Herrman looked questioningly at Herr Meisner. He, in turn, extended his hand to Mike.

"Mister Taylor, I am sure Miss Herrman can provide you with every assistance that you will require. And of course, if there is anything further you wish of me…"

"Of course, Herr Meisner," Mike replied. "And thank you for your interest."

Herr Meisner and Mike shook hands, and then Mike turned and followed Miss Herrman out of the office.

A few moments later, Mike was seated in Miss Herrman's somewhat smaller and more utilitarian office. She looked inquiringly at him, waiting for him to start the conversation.

"Has Herr Meisner told you what I'm looking for?" Mike asked.

He knew his tone was cold and official, so he was not surprised when she adopted the same attitude.

"Only in general terms," she answered. "It has something to do with the Dachau records?" She spoke with only the slightest trace of a German accent. And her voice, though impersonal and businesslike, still retained a high degree of femininity.

"Yes," Mike replied, launching into the cover story he and Craig had decided on, during yesterday's telephone conversation. "Those are the records I want to see. As my government has informed yours, on a top secret priority rating of course, I'm investigating some illegal entries into the United States. There are all rather old cases. But we're making one final effort to clear them up. And some of the people involved might very well have been on the staff at Dachau and other places. I want to try and ferret them out."

"I see," she said.

"Don't you think they should be found out?" Mike asked sharply, irritated by her impersonal tone. "Or should it all be allowed to just die out now!"

As soon as he had spoken, Mike was sorry that he had indulged himself in the luxury of this personal outburst. Just because she rubbed him the wrong way, was no reason to bait her in this manner, he knew. He had too much important work to do with this woman.

But Miss Herrman, after regarding him coldly for a moment, seemed to choose to ignore his remarks. She reached for a pencil and poised it above her pad. "Now, Mister Taylor, if you could be somewhat more specific in your requirements…"

Mike decided to let the incident pass, too. "Well," he began, returning to a more business-like tone, "I want to see the roster of German soldiers assigned to Dachau from 1938 until the war ended. Let's start with the officers. Then, maybe later, I'll want to see the rosters on the enlisted men."

"Even on the officers alone, the number is several hundred," she cautioned him.

"Do you have them designated by whether they're still living?" Mike asked.

She nodded. "Yes. And that reduces the list considerably. But it is still substantial."

"Do you have the lists further refined, in terms of where these people are now? Whether they've been living in Germany all the time since the war? And those officers who have disappeared, but have never been proven dead? That sort of breakdown?"

"I believe we can trace out this information."

"Then that'll help make things simpler, too."

"When do you wish to start?" she asked.

"Right now," Mike answered.

CHAPTER SEVEN

Mike shoved the papers aside and slumped back in his chair. It was several hours later on the same day. Night had come, in fact, as Mike and Miss Herrman had been occupied in compiling the lists of officers who had served at Dachau.

"Well," Mike said, looking at the master tally sheet that he had been keeping during this compilation, "the way I figure it, we've just about covered everyone. Why don't you check me as I read off the totals? Okay?"

"All right," Miss Herrman responded, taking up one of the sheets of paper that had been laying in front of her. "Go ahead."

"Of all the officers who served at Dachau," Mike began, "the records show that 228 of them are still known to definitely be alive. Of these, 184 are living in Germany. That leaves 44 who are living outside of Germany. Now, what do you have on those 44?"

"Twelve of the 44 are known to have gone to South America," Miss Herrman picked up the tally. "That leaves 32. There are 7 that we know are in Egypt, and that leaves us with 25. Of these, 8 have gone to the United States, that we know of. And the remaining 17 are scattered around Europe."

"And then, there are the 34 'untraceables.' The ones who have disappeared entirely," Mike pointed out.

"Do you think the persons you are looking for, are among those 34 'untraceables'?" Miss Herrman asked, referring to the cover story Mike had given her, about his investigating false entries of Germans into the United States.

"Possibly," Mike answered, forcing the optimism into his voice for Miss Herrman's benefit.

Actually, he was discouraged by the results of the officer tally. He had hoped to find some evidence of Behrens being an officer at Dachau, so as to give him a basis for establishing a tie between the man and Kaufman, at the time Kaufman was a prisoner in the camp.

His hopes had gone up, when Miss Herrman had told him that the Dachau records included pictures of all the officers who had served there. And while realizing that looks could change in almost 20 years, whether naturally or by design, Mike had hoped that from among all those pictures, he might spot someone who fit Behrens' description. After all, Behrens was supposedly rather distinctive looking, with his broken nose. But he had found no sign of Behrens, even among the records of the 34 'untraceables.'

"What would you like to check out, next?" Miss Herrman asked.

"Can you make a try at the 34 'untraceables'? And how about the 17 who are now living in other countries in Europe?"

Mike asked. "After all, you never know if any of them might not now be in the United States. Maybe some errors in the records, or something."

"We will check out the 'untraceables' once again. And we will check out those 17, too. But on the 17, I would not hold out much hope for any of them having gone to the United States," Miss Herrman answered. "Our records are very much up to date. We have had to keep them that way, because of the war crime trials."

An unexpected weariness in Miss Hermann's voice made Mike to look across at her. In the night lighting of the office, Miss Herrman's features seemed much softer to Mike than they had earlier in the day. Her face, and especially her eyes, also reflected a deep sadness.

Mike thought, it can't be easy for Germans such as this girl, who was too young to have had a part in World War II, to still have to share the guilt that most of the world directed toward their country.

"And the sins of the fathers shall be vested on the sons, or something along those lines," Mike said softly.

"And on their daughters, too," Miss Herrman added.

"It must get pretty rugged sometimes," Mike said. "I mean, the constant hammering of the world at Germany's guilt."

"It does," she answered, and then she added with defiance, "but we are not looking for pity. Understanding, yes. But not pity."

Mike had a sudden urge, one that surprised him, given his general attitude toward Germans. And even more surprising, he gave voice to that urge. "Miss Herrman," he asked, "how would you like to explain that statement some more, over dinner?"

Less than an hour later, they were seated in the small restaurant that Miss Herrman had suggested. By the time they had arrived there, Mike also had learned that Miss Herrman's first name was Elke. In turn, he had told her his first name, and it was on this basis that they now addressed each other.

"I've got to be honest with you," Mike began, as they had their cocktails before dinner, "my liking for Germans is very limited. You see, I served in the Army, on a concentration camp investigating team. And it was pretty awful." Mike stopped himself at this point. He didn't feel he wanted to tell this girl about his wife Claire, although it was her concentration camp experiences that had most embittered Mike.

Elke sighed. "As much as I would like to, there is nothing I can answer to that. The only answer I can give you, for myself, is a very weak one. But it is the only one I have."

"What is it?"

"When the war ended, I was 8 years old. I had been born in 1937. There is little that I could have done from 1937-1945, to change the war, or to do anything about the concentration camps. Of course, I realize this is only a very personal defense for me, and for me alone. It does not absolve my country, and my people, for what was done."

"What about your parents?" Mike realized the question was a rude one. But he felt he had to know. Perhaps it was because he liked Elke, and he somehow wanted to be able to separate her from the ill feelings he had about Germans in general.

"My parents were killed during the war. My father was a major in the Luftwaffe. Yes," she anticipated the question suggested by Mike's raised eyebrows, "he was a Nazi. A strong one. And he stood for everything that you hate. But he was killed over London, in 1942. When I was 5 years old. And I hardly remember him."

"And your mother?"

"She was a different sort of person, what I remember of her. She was killed in an American bomber raid on Munich, late in the war, in 1945. So, I do remember quite a bit about her. My mother was not a Nazi. She really wasn't anything. She had very few opinions on any subject. She was completely submissive, at first to my father, and then to my grandmother, her mother, with whom we lived during most of the war."

Elke leaned forward and accepted the light Mike offered for her cigarette. "I have thought many times in later years, that perhaps my mother, in her attitude of just going along with everything, was equally as guilty as my father, who was an active Nazi. Does that strike you as odd?"

Mike shook his head. "No. It's the old idea that someone can be just as guilty by omission, as by commission."

"Exactly. And God help me, I don't want to offend the memory of either my mother, or my father. But I believe my mother to be just as guilty as my father. She cannot be excused."

"Is that why you're doing the work you are?" Mike asked. "I mean, all of this work you've been doing in connection with the concentration camps, all of this?"

Elke nodded. "It started out that way, seven years ago, when I first came here to work in the Bureau of Records. What is the English word for it? It was for me, a...a...catharsis?"

"Yes," Mike nodded at the correct word.

"But the guilt feelings are gone now. In fact, they have been gone for several years. Not that I have forgotten what happened. We should never forget. But I feel I can make a greater contribution now, if I am more, how would you put it, more positive about it. Not so much guilty, as more positive. I think that it is up to we younger Germans to prove to the world that we can be good." She smiled wryly. "You might say we are dedicated to disproving the saying that 'the only good German is a dead German.'"

"Do enough Germans feel like you, though?" Mike asked. "It certainly would be wonderful to believe it. But I find it hard to do so."

"We are almost 50 million persons," she said strongly. "And of course everyone does not feel the same way. But that is just what makes it more important for those of us who do really care. We are the ones who have to root out the rotten ones from the war, and to stop any more rotten ones from growing. And that is why I have been doing my work here, for these past seven years."

A thought came to Mike. There was danger involved in it. He

had known Elke only for this one day. But he sensed that she was someone he could trust. And he felt, too, that if he could tell her something of the true purpose of his mission, then perhaps she'd be able to help him in his investigation.

The waiter arrived and began clearing away their cocktail glasses, preparatory to serving dinner. They both grew silent in his presence, and in those few minutes, Mike debated with himself the pros and cons of telling Elke about Behrens.

By the time the waiter served their food, Mike had made up his mind. He wouldn't tell Elke everything. Nothing about who Kaufman was, for example. But he would tell her something of Behrens, of the letters he had written, and of why Mike really was in Frankfurt. Perhaps it could lead them to some new clues for tying Behrens and Kaufman together.

"Elke," he began, "there are some things I want to tell you. But, you've got to promise me you'll keep them in strictest confidence…"

CHAPTER EIGHT

Later in the evening, after putting Elke Herrman into a taxi, Mike returned to his hotel, to find a message from Craig. He had left word for Mike to call. There were two places to try. If it was before 7:00 in the evening, New York time, then Craig could be reached in his office. If after 7:00, then Mike was to put the call into Craig's home.

Since it was 10:30 PM, Frankfurt time, making it 5:30 PM in New York, Mike had instructed the hotel operator to place the call to Craig's office. And now, in his room and lying on the bed, Mike held the telephone to his ear as he listened to the operator completing the circuit. There was a final pause, and then Craig's voice came on the line.

"Taylor?"

Mike smiled. The old bastard was just the same, whether you sat across from him in his office, or talked to him, over 3,000 miles of telephone cable. No preliminaries, no time wasted on greetings. Just barebones essentials.

"Yes, I'm here," Mike answered.

"What've you found out so far?"

"Well, I've only been here today," Mike pointed out. "I've started with a check on the officers who were stationed at Dachau during the war."

"Anything on that list to tie Behrens to it?"

"Not yet," Mike admitted. "But there are several 'untraceables' on the officer list, and I'll be checking those out. I'll also be going into the enlisted men's lists."

"Frankly, I think you're wasting your time," Craig said. "I told you yesterday that I had reservations about this whole side trip. And I'm getting more doubtful by the minute. I don't think you'll find a damn thing in Frankfurt."

"But Chief, it's at least worth a try," Mike countered. "I'm not done here, so don't count it out yet."

"Well, I'm going to count it out, soon enough," Craig said. "Time's getting short. And I think you're better off going to the other cities -- to Milan, Florence and Paris -- to see if you can tie Behrens to the letters that were written from those cities."

"Yes. Sure, I have to do that," Mike agreed. "but all that is still just circumstantial. And if Behrens is ever confronted with it, he can deny it all. What I'm after here, though, he couldn't deny. A real tie between him and Kaufman! After all, Kaufman spent three years as a prisoner in Dachau. And I think the chances are good that the letter writer dates back to those days. And if I can tie in Behrens to the camp, then I figure we'll be that much better off. The way I see it, our State Department's going to have a rough enough time convincing the Italian government, or the German government, or whatever government gets involved, to do anything, anyway. And the stronger a case we can build, the better it will be."

"Yes," Craig had to admit. "I agree that the more specific a case we can build, the better it will be. But still, we don't want to cut this thing too fine. We've got to produce something for the State Department. And fast. And if all we can end up giving the Department is evidence of the tie between Behrens and the letter writing, then that'll have to be it."

"Can I have some more time here, though?" Mike asked. "I really feel it might be worthwhile," he added strongly.

"Okay," Craig said grudgingly. "But no more than two days. And then, no matter what, you hustle your rear end back to the other cities. You got that?"

"Yes," Mike assured him.

"Goodbye," Craig said, and hung up at his end.

Mike looked at the dead receiver in amusement. What a guy. He wondered if Craig ever spoke to his wife or kids in anything other than abrupt tones.

CHAPTER NINE

As Mike entered the Bureau of Records library the next morning, he saw that Elke had already arrived. She was seated at a table concentrating on a file, while several more files were stacked around her.

Elke did not hear Mike come in. He stood in the doorway for a moment and looked at her, a slight smile on his lips. He had to admit that Elke certainly was one German on whom his old rule of dislike didn't fit very well.

Elke sensed his presence and looked up, smiling a greeting. "Good morning. How are you this morning?"

"Fine," Mike answered, walking to the table and looking at the files. "You've been busy."

"Well, I thought I would get started on a few things, while I waited for you." She reached for a piece of paper and read from it. "I have started tracers on the 17 Dachau officers whose records show they are living in different parts of Europe. Information on them should begin coming in shortly, at least in the cases of the ones living in the bigger cities.

And I have also put in a request that a renewed search be made for the 34 'untraceables,' though I have to admit that this is a very faint hope. And," she added waving at that stacks of files surrounding her, "I have obtained these records of the enlisted men at Dachau. I was beginning to sort them out, when you came in."

Mike looked at his watch. It was only 9:20 AM. "You've been a very busy girl. What time did you get here?"

"Oh," Elke said, shrugging her shoulders. "I'm an early riser."

"Yeah, so what time were you here?" Mike persisted.

"About 7:00," she admitted.

Mike looked at her in appreciation.

"Well," she asked with a smile, "shall we get to work on these lists?"

....

"I thought we could use some coffee."

Elke's voice cut in on Mike's concentration. He looked up, and at the doorway as she came into the library, carrying a tray with a coffee pot, two cups and some cookies.

"How right you are," Mike agreed, pushing his chair back from the table and stretching.

He looked at his watch. "It's 6:30. You must be beat. Almost 12 hours at this. Why don't you go home?"

"Well, you must be tired, also," Elke countered.

"At least I have not had to look at those hundreds of records all day, without hardly ever stopping."

Elke nodded toward the stacks of files. "Have you found anything yet?"

Mike shook his head. "No. Not really. There are a few very vague possibilities, where the descriptions or pictures bear a slight resemblance. But nothing much."

Elke poured coffee for them, and then sat down opposite Mike. "What now?" she asked.

Mike shrugged. "On to the other cities, I suppose. These are all personnel records from Dachau?"

"All of them."

"Then it was a wild goose chase. Just like Craig said it would be."

"Craig?"

"The name of my boss," Mike explained. "He thought my coming to Frankfurt was useless in the first place. He said I wouldn't find anything here. And it looks like he was right."

"I would imagine, however, that in an investigation of this type, it is necessary to check out everything? One never knows what can be found on, what did you call it, a wild goose chase?"

Mike laughed. "Hell, you could almost call this whole investigation a wild goose chase. It's the weirdest thing I've ever been on."

"Oh?" Elke asked, and then busied herself reaching for the pot and pouring herself some more coffee.

The night before, Mike had told Elke only some of the bare essentials of the investigation. And it was obvious now, that although she was naturally curious to know more, her good manners prevented her from asking questions.

Mike realized this, as he looked at Elke. And aware that he'd be leaving the next day, he decided she was entitled to know more about the case she had been working on, so devotedly, these last two days. And besides, he felt he could trust her completely.

"I guess you're entitled to know what this thing is all about, Elke." Mike began.

"You don't have to," Elke interrupted. "really…"

"No, it's okay," Mike assured her. "I'm sure the information is safe enough with you. And besides, I want you to know. I feel you deserve to know, after all the work you've put in on this thing."

Elke smiled at him. "Well," she admitted, "I cannot say that I have not been almost eaten up with curiosity, to know everything about the investigations."

Mike smiled back at her as he began his explanation. "Remember last night, I told you I was looking for the records of a man called Behrens? And that the reason I was looking for him was that some threats had been made on the life of an American citizen? And that we had reason to believe this Behrens was making the threats, and that Behrens had been an officer assigned to Dachau? That's pretty much all I told you, right?"

"Yes."

"Okay. Now, here's the full story. You see, there's this

American Jew, who at one time was a German national. He was put in Dachau, but he managed to survive the war, and later, he emigrated to the U.S. In the years since, he's become a very successful and highly respected person. He's not only become wealthy as an importer of art goods, but he's also become very active politically. Not so that the public would know, though. He's more of a behind-the-scenes man, a real, but almost unknown power in the Democratic Party. So far, it sounds like a lovely and successful sequel to a rotten time during the war, doesn't it?"

"Yes."

"Well, the happy story started having some sour notes in it, as of about two months ago."

"What happened?"

"The man started receiving threatening letters. Letters that appeared to be from a German. Anti-Semitic letters that threatened he and his family with death. So far, there've been four of the letters. All mailed from Europe. The last one came about two weeks ago."

"How awful."

"And that's only part of it. The man's daughter is going to be married soon. It's his stepdaughter, really. The man and his present wife were married after the war. You see, his first wife died in Dachau. The other woman, the one he married after the war, she and her daughter had been at Auschwitz. They survived. The daughter was just a kid when the war ended. But the husband had been killed."

"Oh God," Elke murmured.

"These letters, of course, have had a terrible effect on the man. To have survived Dachau. And now to be faced with this. And to add to the problem, the daughter had a severe mental breakdown several years ago, as a result of what happened during the war. She spent three years in a sanitarium, and she's only been well for a couple of years. The father is afraid that she'll become ill again, if she ever finds out about these threatening letters."

"And the mother?"

"She doesn't know anything. So far, it's only the father who knows. And he's the one who has asked for help in tracking down the source of the letters.

"And there also are political reasons. You see, everyone's worried about the effect this would have on the question of German re-armament, if the facts come out, about how an American survivor of Dachau is now being threatened by a German. It would be bad, of course."

"Who cares about such political things!" Elke said bitterly.

"I couldn't agree with you more." Mike sighed. "But I guess we've got to be realistic. I don't like to admit it, but we've got to."

Elke sipped her coffee. "And it is this Behrens, whom you believe to be the German, who is writing the threatening letters. And as you told me last night, you were hoping to find some record here of Behrens, so that you could tie him to the man who was the prisoner in Dachau."

"Right." Mike fished in his briefcase. "I've told you so much,

Elke, you might as well learn everything. Here are photostats of the four threatening letters. On one of them, the Rome postmarked one, I've been able to trace the typewriter on which it was written, to the hotel in Rome, where Behrens used to live. And now, when I leave Frankfurt, I'll go on to the other three cities – Milan, Florence and Paris – and try to do the same thing. It's a tenuous tie, but the best thing we have so far. And time's growing short."

Elke took the four letters and started to read them. Mike watched her, and for an instant, he had some self-doubts about having told her so much. But then, as he looked at Elke, he realized that he had come to trust her implicitly, even in this short period of time. It was only a feeling, he admitted, but he was sure about it.

When Elke finished the last of the letters, Mike reached out to take them back. But Elke didn't notice his extended hand. She seemed lost in thought as she shuffled the letters in her hands, first examining one, and then another.

"This one descriptive phrase in here," she said wonderingly. "The one that is in all the letters…"

"You mean the one that goes, 'a good German who knows he must kill you to save the world from Jewish financial and political domination?'" Mike asked.

"Yes…"

"What about it?"

"I feel I have heard it somewhere, before."

"You probably have," Mike agreed. "It was a common enough sentiment in Germany during the 30's and the war."

"Yes, yes, I know," Elke answered impatiently. "But just those exact words. I have heard just those exact words before."

"Probably something similar in one of Hitler's speeches?" Mike suggested.

"No," Elke said. "Where was it? Where was it?"

Mike leaned forward, his interest heightened. "The exact words, Elke? The exact same words as appeared in the letters?"

"I didn't hear them," Elke said thoughtfully. And then she grew excited. "I read them. Yes. That's it. I read them!"

"Maybe in some of your cataloguing work?" Mike offered.

"Yes… that's probably where." Elke tapped her fingers on the edge of the table as she concentrated, trying to recall the source of the phrase. "It was in connection with Dachau," she said finally. "Of that, I am sure."

"In connection with Dachau? Where? In some records? In a book you read?"

"No…it wasn't in any of those. It was in something more… more personal…"

"More personal?" Mike echoed. "Maybe a letter?"

"No!" Elke exclaimed. "It was in a diary! A partially burned diary that was salvaged from the stove in one of the German officers' barracks at Dachau. I am sure of it!"

"Elke, do you know where that diary is now?"

CHAPTER TEN

"Here it is," Elke said, bringing a file box to a table near where Mike was standing.

They were in another library, elsewhere in the same building. This room, it was obvious from its musty odor, was used mainly to store records that were needed infrequently.

"I am sure it is in this file," Elke said, as she took out a packet of pages bound by two rubber bands. "This is the diary, or what is left of it."

"Let's take the bands off and spread the pages on the table," Mike suggested.

"Yes," Elke agreed. She removed the rubber bands and started to spread the first pages on the table. "As I recall, the pages that were not burned, covered the period from late 1942 until approximately the time that Dachau was being liberated. It was mainly the first part of the diary that was burned."

"Uh huh," Mike said as they examined the pages. "Is there an owner's name, or anything like that?"

"No. That part was destroyed.

It was probably at the beginning of the book." She looked at him. "Can you read the German?" she asked.

Mike nodded. "I learned as part of my work during the war." He turned his attention again to the diary. "Let's see if we can find the phrase in here. Do you recall about where it was?"

"It was in many places," Elke answered. "That is why I remembered it. Because the writer repeated it so often. Like a credo or slogan. It started appearing almost from the very beginning."

Mike began turning over the first pages that still remained in the partially destroyed diary. At about the fifth page, under the date of October 18, 1942, he let out an exclamation. "Wait! Here it is!"

"See? Didn't I tell you?" Elke said excitedly. "The same phrase!"

The phrase was contained in the last paragraph of the entry for that day. Mike began to read aloud, translating the writing into English. "Today," the paragraph started, "the news of the war is good. We are winning our cause on all fronts. And here, too, there is only good news to report. We are constantly increasing our capacity for dealing with the Jews. I know that Auschwitz has much the greater reputation for destroying Jews. But we are certainly catching up. And I am right in the middle of it, a good German who knows he must kill Jews to save the world from their financial and political domination. Yes, if we are given enough time, we can certainly rid the world of this plague. Oh, oh. There is Hans, knocking at the door. That means it is time for my bath.

What would I do without Hans? He is the perfect aide. Alert, and completely dedicated to me. And now, I must go, or the bath will cool."

Mike put down the page. "It's certainly the same," he agreed. "Except for a couple of understandable changes in the use of nouns and pronouns, it's exactly the same phrase." He looked up from the page and spoke to Elke. "You say there's more?"

"It appeared many times," she said.

Mike began skimming through the pages. The writing was large, very neat and in a clear, firm hand. So it was easy to skim, while looking for the key phrase. The next time he spotted it was about fifteen pages later, under an entry marked December 30, 1942.

Again, he began to read aloud. "Today, on the eve of the New Year, Hans and I had ourselves a special treat with the Jews. He selected two of the strongest, most fit looking, stripped them bare, and set them outside. It was 22 degrees, and all of the snow was ice-covered. I told the Jews that one of them would be allowed inside again. But only one. The other would have to stay outside, and would of course freeze to death. And I told them it was up to them to decide who would come in. Then, Hans gave them each a large knife. We had carefully chosen these two, to make sure they did not know each other, and were not friends. Thus, the stage was set. By reason of my ultimatum, they immediately were enemies, and each knew he would have to kill the other, in order to survive. The battle went on for almost six minutes.

And then, in one of those quirks of battle, each stabbed the other, fatally. So, neither survived. But it is just as well. As a good German who knows he must kill Jews to save the world from their financial and political domination, I must admit this coincidence to have been a welcome one. Two Jews dead, for the price of one. Yes, for both my trusted aide, Hans, and myself, the diversion was a propitious one, to herald the New Year. How can 1943 help but be a good year, after so promising a sign?"

"Oh, my God," Elke whispered, horrified. "Such animals! I am so ashamed for them!"

"I couldn't agree with you more," Mike said grimly. He tapped the page which contained the entry he had just read. "You know, there are several things that become obvious out of all this."

"The possibility that Behrens and the diary's writer are the same person?" Elke guessed.

"Yes," Mike said. "That's the most important thing. I'll admit it's reaching a bit to come to that conclusion. But damn it! The similarity between this writer's use of that phrase, and the wording of the phrase in the letters to Kaufman, well, they're just too coincidental to dismiss."

"You said there are other things that are obvious. What are they?" Elke asked.

"Well, for one thing, even though the diary was found in the stove in one of the officer barracks, there was still the possibility that it actually was some enlisted man's diary. But now that we've looked at its contents, I think we can safely conclude that it was an officer who wrote it."

"What else?"

"These references the officer makes to his aide, Hans. Hans and the diary writer seem to have been very close. Perhaps there's some indication in the personnel rosters about an enlisted man, with the first name of Hans, whose duties were as an aide to an officer? If we could find anything like that, then we might be able to trace Hans down. Then, through him, we'd be able to establish if this diary writer, and Behrens, are in fact the same person!"

"And then, if you could definitely establish that the diary writer is Behrens, you would be able to place him as being in Dachau at the same time as Kaufman!" Elke added with growing excitement.

"Exactly," Mike answered. "And that would give the rest of my case a stronger base, for use by the State Department. It might be just the link I'd need, to establish some logic as to how, after all these years, Behrens suddenly picks Kaufman out of the air, and starts terrorizing him with these letters. It's all circumstantial, I know. But it begins to build a good case."

"I will start checking the enlisted men's personnel rosters at once," Elke said with determination.

"Hold on a second," Mike stopped her. "Do you recall any other appearances of that phrase? Anywhere in this diary?"

"Yes. As I remember, there were several."

"Let's look some more, then," Mike said, bending over the table and resuming his skimming of the pages.

As the moments went by, Mike found five more examples of the phrase on widely scattered dates in early and late 1943, and in late 1944. Then, as he started to turn a page containing an entry for February 17, 1945, Mike suddenly stopped and began to examine the entry closely.

"What is it?" Elke asked, noticing Mike's interest.

"It looks like our friend is having some second thoughts about the outcome of the war," Mike commented. "Listen to this."

He began to read the entry of February 17, 1945. "Due to what I am sure must be temporary circumstances, I found it necessary today to institute the plan Hans and I have discussed over the past several weeks. At my direction, Hans brought the rabbi to my office this afternoon. And it is good that Hans and I kept him from the ovens."

"What?" Elke said unbelievingly. "You mean he wants to save the Jews now?"

"No. He seems to have something else in mind. Listen."

Mike picked up the narrative of the entry. "Yes, it is good we saved the life of this Jew, because he seems to be the only rabbi left in all of Dachau. And we definitely need this rabbi for our plan. Hah! The rabbi's face was a sight to see, when I told him that I wanted him to instruct Hans and myself in how to be Jews. He looked at me as if I were crazy. Of course, I didn't tell him the reason.

Not only because, as a Jew he has no right to know, but more important, because only Hans and I must know the reason. The

74

others would not understand. It is not that I do not believe in our Fuhrer and the Fatherland. It is just that I like to think of myself as a pragmatist. And I like to be certain of the possibilities of future events, and to have prepared myself for all eventualities."

"What is he talking about?" Elke interrupted impatiently.

"Here, this explains it," Mike said.

He began reading again. "That is why I have decided to learn all there is to know about Judaism. In this way, if the war ends badly for us, it will be possible for me to pass myself off as a Jew, until I can escape from Germany. After all, everything will be so confused at that time, that I can simply assume the records and identity of one of the Jews who has been gassed. Of course, I have brought Hans into this with me. He has been a loyal aide to me, and I feel I can repay him in this manner. As our first step, we already have acquired the papers of two Jews who have been gassed. It took several weeks for Hans to sort through the files, but he found exactly the right papers. In both cases, the persons physically resembled us. And each of them was without family, so Hans and I will be free of any possible embarrassment of family reunions."

"He thinks of everything, the monster," Elke said.

Mike continued reading. "And today, I started step two. The instruction of Hans and myself in the Jewish faith. Ah, how surprised the rabbi was, when I told him why I wanted to see him. His name is Rabbi Dov Levin, a German Jew. He, of course, was not very happy when I told him he would have to instruct Hans and me. He is a smart fellow, this rabbi, to give him credit, and staunch in character. But when I told him I would spare the lives of his wife and two young daughters, who also are in Dachau, if he instructed Hans and me, then he bent somewhat. I have warned him, too, that if he grows lax in his instruction of us, his family will immediately be put to death. And so, our instruction in Judaism has started. It is disgusting for me to have to study the miserable ways of these scum Jews. And to think about assuming the identity of a Jew. But it is only a temporary expedient. And one must be pragmatic, mustn't one…"

Mike shook his head. "He calls it pragmatism. What a miserable sub-human."

"It is awful," Elke agreed. "That poor rabbi."

Mike resumed his search through the diary. As the pages went by they found additional references in the succeeding months after February of 1945, to the writer's dealings with the rabbi. They came finally to the last entry in the diary. Mike read it aloud.

"There are only hours, perhaps only moments left, until the Americans arrive. Just a short while ago, one of their airplanes flew in low over the camp. If we only had anti-aircraft weapons, we would have shown him! Well, no matter, now. All is lost for the Fatherland. Ach! I must stop using words like Fatherland.

In fact, I must stop thinking like a German, because in just a few moments, both Hans and I will walk out of this camp and become temporary Jews. Our preparations are all completed. Our Jewish identity papers, and our old clothes are packed into my brief case. When we leave the camp, we will go deep into the woods. And we will remain there for at least a week or two. We will eat only what we can find, which should be only berries and the like. In this way, by the time we emerge from the woods, we should look badly enough beaten in body to pass as inmates of the camp. Then, we can tell the Americans that we escaped from a camp just before the Germans retreated. And we will explain our relatively healthy bodies by saying we only just arrived in Dachau several weeks ago. If all goes well after that, we should eventually be able to make our way out of Germany, and shed this Jewish sham of ours. We can then become Aryans again."

"Is there nothing this beast does not think of?" Elke said with frustration. "Is he so sure of everything?"

"Almost," Mike answered, his voice suddenly mounting in excitement. "Almost," he repeated, "but it looks here like he messed up on one thing."

"What is that?"

"Listen." Mike picked up the narrative of the entry. "Yes, the plan is good. And it is complete, except for one detail. Rabbi Dov Levin is still alive, and he is nowhere to be found. Hans is out searching for him right now. But I am certain the Jew has escaped from the camp. And no wonder. Almost all of the guards are deserting. If the Jews were not so weakened, they would probably attack the few of us who are left. Well, it was a stupid error, killing the Rabbi's wife and daughters in full view of those other prisoners. I should have realized the prisoners would have gotten word to the rabbi. And then, of course, he must have realized that I am going to kill him, too, since I had no further use for him. So, he escaped. It is not good. But nothing can be done about it. And now, I really must get started. I see Hans returning. And it is time for us to leave. I will have to burn this diary now, of course. Perhaps it has been silly for me to have kept up the entries knowing as I have for some time that I would have to destroy the diary. But on the other hand, when I am able to write things down like this, it helps me to think clearly, and to plan carefully. And clear thinking and careful planning have been so necessary these past months. But now, it is time. Here, now, is Hans, and we must go. A bitter joke, it is, that we go as Jews. But, one must be pragmatic about it. It is the way life is constituted. Heil Hitler!"

Mike turned over the last page. "Wow," he muttered. "It's fantastic."

"Yes," Elke agreed.

Mike remained silent a moment, thinking. Then he spoke. "Let me just reason a few things out loud, okay?"

"Okay."

He picked up a page of the diary and read it. "A good German knows he must kill the Jews to save the world from their financial and political domination." Mike put the page back on the table. "The way the diary writer says it there, and the way it's said in the letters to Kaufman, are almost exactly alike. Now, from that, I think we could draw a pretty fair conclusion that it is the same person doing the writing in both cases. That person being Behrens."

"But Behrens isn't passing himself off as a Jew, is he?" Elke asked.

Mike nodded. "I thought of that. No, he isn't. But hell, the diary writer said his Jewish identity would only be temporary, until he could get out of Germany."

"True."

"Now," Mike continued, "there's another way we might possibly be able to establish definitely if this diary writer is Behrens. And that's through this aide of his. Hans. The one he keeps referring to in so many of his entries."

"And I have already started tracing this Hans out, on the enlisted men's rosters," Elke said.

"Right. But then, there's also another possibility. And it may be the really big one."

"What is that?" Elke asked.

"The rabbi," Mike answered.

"The rabbi?" she repeated.

"You bet." Mike leaned forward and spoke with intensity. "Elke, in that diary, the writer said the rabbi escaped. Couldn't it be possible that he's still alive?"

Elke thought a moment. "Yes...but that depends of course on his age in 1945. Almost twenty years have passed."

"He probably wasn't too old," Mike mused. "Remember, when the diary writer first mentioned the rabbi, he said he'd spare the lives of his wife and young daughters. So, he probably wasn't too old, then. Now, what I want to know is this. Do you think it might be possible to trace that rabbi? To find out if he's still alive, and if so, where he is today?"

"I will have to get in touch with some other research and record departments," Elke thought aloud.

"You can't tell them too much," Mike warned. "In fact, you can't tell them hardly anything."

"I know. I will manage. But it will take a day. Two days. Possibly three."

"Make it a day," Mike ordered. "Craig is breathing too heavily on me, already."

CHAPTER ELEVEN

Elke put a top priority rating on the tracer request she sent out on the rabbi. Despite this, it took almost two days before she received any word. As soon as she had read the information, Elke called Mike at his hotel.

"We have found him," she announced triumphantly.

"The rabbi?"

"Yes. We have found him. And he is alive."

"Where?"

"In Paris. In a Jewish Shelter home."

"Great. Then Paris it'll be."

"I will drive you to the airport."

Mike looked at his watch. "Then be here in an hour."

After speaking with Elke, Mike had called Frankfurt Airport and had made a reservation on the 10:20 AM flight to Paris. He had packed hurriedly, and checked out of the hotel, just in time to meet Elke.

Now, at the airport, they were seated in the passenger lounge, awaiting the call for Mike to board.

"Do you think the rabbi will really be able to help you?" Elke asked.

"I'm hoping he'll be able to tell me the name of the person who wrote that diary."

"But the German officer must have changed his name after the war," Elke pointed out.

"I'm sure of that," Mike agreed. "But even if we have his old name, then you can trace him in your records. And I would be surprised if that trace didn't eventually lead right back to Behrens."

"You are fairly positive he is the one, aren't you?"

"It's all circumstantial," Mike admitted. "But it looks pretty good to me." He thought for a moment. "And then, too, I'm hoping the rabbi can give me a description of the diary writer. That'll really tie it up in a nice bundle."

"If the description is that of Behrens," Elke stressed.

"If the description is that of Behrens," Mike agreed.

They were silent for a moment, then Elke spoke. "You will let me know what happens, when you see the rabbi?"

Her voice sounded strained, and Mike turned to look at her. She smiled in response, but the expression was tentative and unsure.

Mike took her hand. "We'll see each other again, Elke." He said softly. Her hand, which had grasped his only lightly, now responded with a greater intensity.

Mike's flight was announced, and they rose and walked to the boarding gate. "I'll call you tonight," he told Elke, leaning forward and quickly kissing her. Then he turned and walked through the gate.

Looking at Mike's retreating back, Elke smiled as she felt the warmth of their first kiss spread through her body. But suddenly, she was thrown off balance, when a man bumped into her as he rushed to the boarding gate.

She looked after the man, her face momentarily reflecting annoyance at his bad manners. Then she smiled. No, she shouted silently toward the man, who was short, dressed in a gray suit, and walked with a limp, not even you, you rude little man, can make me angry at this moment. I am happy. I am truly happy!

CHAPTER TWELVE

Elke had been able to trace the rabbi to the Jewish Welfare Committee, an international organization set up at the end of the war, to help relocate the displaced Jews of Europe. Working through the Committee, Elke learned that the rabbi was living in Paris, under the care of a local Shelter for Homeless Jews. This organization maintained hundreds of needy Jews in a poor section of Montmartre. And the Shelter had acknowledged Elke's tracer, and informed her that the rabbi known as Dov Levin was under its care. All of this information, Elke had given to Mike on the way to the airport.

Later that same day, he had been told that Rabbi Levin was living in a small apartment in a building near the Shelter. The person Mike spoke to, had given him the address. And now, as Mike left his hotel and walked into the Place du Comedie Francais, toward a taxi stand, he folded the piece of paper containing the address, and placed it in his pocket.

There were no taxis at the stand, so Mike had to wait for one to come down the Rue St. Honore or the Avenue de L'Opera.

While waiting, he had a moment to look at his surroundings. As always happened when he visited Paris, Mike felt at ease. Paris affected him in a good way. He glanced over at the gleaming Comedie Francais, cleanly sandblasted by De Gaulle's edict, as were most of the other public buildings in the city. There were those, Mike knew, who felt Paris was a cold, a sullen city. But to him, it had always been a warm place.

He spotted a taxi coming off the Avenue De L'Opera, and he hailed it. The cab veered off the avenue and pulled up to the taxi stand. Mike climbed in, and gave the driver the rabbi's address.

A short time later, he stepped from the taxi, in front of the rabbi's address. Located on one of the side streets almost within the shadows of the Sacre Coeur, the building was only four stories high. In keeping with its surroundings, it was shabby and ill kept. Just this side of being a slum, Mike thought, as he glanced up and down the small street. Several store signs in Hebrew met his glance, signifying what he already knew, that this was an almost totally Jewish section of Paris, similar in makeup to New York's famed Lower East Side, though much smaller.

The rabbi, Mike had been informed, lived in apartment 3-B, which, in European terms, meant the fourth floor. Mike entered the building, hoping for an elevator, but expecting none. His hope was unfulfilled, but his expectation was, so Mike began climbing the narrow staircase. Shortly, he reached the fourth floor. It was in almost total darkness, the one hall light having a difficult time fighting the late afternoon gloom.

Mike knocked on the door for 3-B. No answer, so he knocked again. Still no answer. Cautiously, he tried the door knob. It turned in his hand. Mike pushed the door open and looked into the room.

At the far end, framed in the outline of the window, he saw a figure, motionless, silent. He started to address the person, whom he assumed to be Rabbi Dov Levin. But then he realized that the rabbi was praying. Mike recalled from his War Crimes work, that Orthodox Jews prayed at dusk each day.

Silently, he entered the room and closed the door behind him. As he waited for the Rabbi to finish his prayers, Mike looked around the room, which was poorly lighted by one floor lamp.

Even the deep shadows of evening failed to fill the obvious emptiness of the barren little apartment. There were a couple of plain chairs, a tiny table, and off in one corner, a cot. The window where the rabbi was standing and praying, his back to Mike, was the only one in the room. Off to one side, there was an open doorway, and through it, Mike could see a small Pullman kitchen.

Completing his examination of the apartment, Mike returned his attention to the rabbi, whose body was swaying back and forth in the traditional movement of a Jew in prayer. Rabbi Levin seemed as poorly kept as his surroundings. He had a slight, bent body. And he was wearing badly fitting clothes which hung in a way that accentuated his frailty.

Mike wondered if the rabbi had heard his knock, and was aware of his presence in the room.

The rabbi took three steps backward, which seemed to signify the end of his prayer. Then, slowly, he turned and looked across the room at Mike.

"Vas vilst du?" he asked in Yiddish. "What do you want?" His voice was small and distant, the words just barely escaping through his thin and almost motionless lips.

Mike was shocked at the rabbi's appearance. Although the Shelter people had told Mike that Rabbi Levin was only 58 years old, he appeared to be at least in his 70's. His thin, lined face was framed in a scraggly white beard. He kept his hands one in the other, across his breast, ceaselessly twining and untwining them.

But it was the rabbi's eyes that sent a cold shudder through Mike. They were dull and empty, reflecting nothing of either the man or his surroundings.

"Vas vilst du?" the rabbi repeated in the same small voice.

Mike had been told by the Shelter that the rabbi understood English. And since his knowledge of Yiddish was non-existent, and his French was hardly better, Mike addressed the other man in English.

"Are you Rabbi Dov Levin?"

The rabbi nodded almost imperceptibly. But he didn't speak. Instead, he shuffled to the cot in the corner of the room and sat down, his hands in his lap, his legs together and his head bowed. He seemed hardly aware of Mike's presence.

Mike took one of the chairs and carried it near the cot.
He sat down and looked at the rabbi. "I...I would like to talk with you for a few moments..." he began.

The rabbi gave no sign that he heard Mike.

"You are Rabbi Dov Levin, aren't you?" Mike asked, already sure of the man's identity, but hoping to get some verbal response. It was becoming obvious to Mike that the rabbi was only remotely in touch with his surroundings.

Again, the rabbi nodded slightly, but he still did not speak.

Mike decided to try another approach. "Is there anything I can get you? Perhaps a glass of water from the kitchen? Or would you like a cigarette?" He pulled a pack from his pocket and offered it to the rabbi.

The man ignored both Mike and the cigarettes. He continued to sit on the cot, motionless, head down. Then, just as Mike was concluding that a conversation was impossible, Rabbi Levin spoke.

"You…you are…American?" he asked, turning his saddened eyes in Mike's direction.

"Yes."

The rabbi's eyes held Mike's for an instant, but then the man looked down again, away from Mike.

Quickly, Mike tried to extend the tiny thread of conversation. "Do you know any Americans? Have you met any of us before?" he asked. The questions were inane and empty, he knew, but he was grasping at anything, hoping to draw the rabbi out of his shell and into a conversation.

Rabbi Levin looked up again, but not at Mike. Instead, he stared across the room, seemingly seeing nothing. "Americans are good," he said slowly, tonelessly. "Americans are good."

"You like Americans? You've met Americans before?"

The rabbi looked at Mike. "You are an American soldier?" he asked. "American soldier is good." He nodded. "American soldier is good."

"When did you meet American soldiers?" Mike asked, reasoning that the rabbi probably was recalling the American soldiers who had liberated Dachau. If this was the rabbi's thought process, then Mike wanted to reinforce it, and draw him into a conversation about that time period. Then, Mike hoped, he'd be able to work the conversation around to the rabbi's time in Dachau, and to the writer of the diary. Mike repeated his question. "When did you meet American soldiers?"

The rabbi did not answer right away. He seemed to be struggling with his thoughts. Mike waited, until the rabbi spoke. His words were slow and halting.

"They…were so good…to me. The American soldiers. They were…so good to me. They were…so good to me. They were…so good to me…"

The rabbi repeated the same words, each time more softly, until he trailed off into silence. It seemed to Mike that the man was incapable of maintaining any flow of logical thought. Mike's hopes of learning anything from the rabbi began to ebb, but he decided to keep trying.

"Did you meet the American soldiers…at…at Dachau?" He asked cautiously, worried as to what effect the name of the concentration camp might have on the rabbi.

"Soldiers? At Dachau?" Rabbi Levin repeated. The name of the camp didn't seem to affect him adversely. "Yes," he nodded, "the American soldiers. Dachau. Yes. Yes. The American soldiers. Yes."

"You were in Dachau, weren't you?" Mike interrupted the rabbi's mumblings. "You were in Dachau many years ago?"

Rabbi Levin had begun swaying back and forth on his cot, the upper part of his body in a slow, constant forward-backward movement. He clasped his hands closer to his breast.

"Yes. Dachau. Yes," he repeated.

"Do you remember the officer and his aide?" Mike asked tensely.

The rabbi's face contorted in misery and his swaying increased in intensity. "May God forgive me," he cried softly. "For them, may God forgive me."

"Do you remember that they wanted you to teach them how to be Jewish? Do you remember that?" Mike asked gently, but insistently.

"Do you remember that?"

"What could I do?" the rabbi cried out. "What could I do? They said they would kill Sarah and the children. What could I do?"

"Of course," Mike reassured him.

Rabbi Levin was crying now, the tears sliding down his wrinkled face. Mike wanted to stop asking his questions, sensing how painful it was for the rabbi. But he forced himself to go on.

He was so close now. So close to what he had to find out.

"What could I do?" Rabbi Levin repeated with sorrow. "What could I do? God, what could I do?"

"What was the name of the officer?" Mike asked. "Rabbi Levin, what was the name of the officer? The one you taught to be Jewish?'"

For a moment, Rabbi Levin continued to cry, and to sway back and forth. And then, as Mike watched, the man seemed to change almost totally in outward behavior. His body stopped swaying, and his tears ceased. His hands no longer clasped and unclasped. Even his breathing grew quite still.

Mike leaned forward and looked closely at Rabbi Levin. He shook his head in resignation. The rabbi had withdrawn deep into his own troubled thoughts, had broken his immediate contact with reality.

He is like a dead man, Mike thought to himself. Like a vegetable. Just sitting there. Existing. But being nothing. Gently, Mike shook Rabbi Levin's shoulder. No response. No change. The face remained expressionless. The eyes hardly blinked.

Reluctantly, Mike stood up. To question the rabbi further, he knew, would be useless. Obviously, the man had built an emotional wall, a barricade, against the memories of Dachau. Up to a point, he seemed capable of thinking about the camp, that point being his willingness to flagellate himself with his guilty feelings. But beyond that, the rabbi seemed incapable of communicating. And Mike recognized this fact in the rabbi's present withdrawn state.

Mike looked down at the bowed and motionless figure. So sad, he thought. So sad and so cruel. A life without living. A soul without identity.

Silently, he walked from the room.

CHAPTER THIRTEEN

When Mike reached his hotel a short while later, there was a message waiting. Elke had called from Frankfurt, and had left word for him to return the call.

Mike told the concierge to place the call, and within a few moments after he had entered his room, the telephone rang. It was Elke.

"Mike? Is that you?" she asked, after he had picked up the receiver.

"It sure is," Mike answered, happy at the sound of her voice. "It's good to hear something pleasant, for a change. It's been a very depressing afternoon."

"Didn't you find the rabbi?"

"Yes. I found him. But it didn't do much good."

"What do you mean?"

"I mean, he couldn't tell me anything."

"Oh."

"It was terrible, Elke. Just terrible. He...well...he was just a shell of a man.

And I felt like such a bastard, even asking him any questions."

"It must have been awful. But you say you did ask him questions. What happened then? He did not want to answer them?"

"It wasn't a matter of not wanting to answer. He couldn't. He just couldn't. It was like he had built a wall around what had happened at Dachau. He obviously felt guilty as hell. And beyond a certain point, he couldn't remember anything. And that included the identity of the officer and his aide."

"The poor man," Elke said.

"Yes, the poor man. I hope you never see anything like it, Elke. It…it was shocking." With an effort, Mike tore his thoughts from the rabbi and asked Elke, "Hey, what about the aide? Were you able to trace him down? Learn his identity?"

"No. I'm afraid not yet," Elke answered. "But I am still working on it. And I am sure I will have something, soon," she added hopefully.

"Thanks for the encouragement," Mike said wryly. "But the truth of the matter is, you haven't been able to find anything, yet. And you probably won't be able to. Right?"

There was a pause at the other end of the lin. "Well, yes, Mike. You are right," Elke admitted. "I cannot find any trace of him. I have tried many sources. But it is no good. I cannot find any trace of the aide."

"Damn," Mike explained. "What a dead-end day this has turned out to be!"

"What will you do now?" Elke asked.

"Well, tomorrow morning, I'll check the Hotel Montpensier. That's the one Behrens stayed at in Paris. And I'll see if he was registered there at the time the letter was sent from Paris to Kaufman."

"And if the two dates are the same?"

"Then I'll go on to Milan and Florence, and check Behrens out in those cities."

"I hope you have better success tomorrow, than you did today," Elke said.

"I hope so, too," Mike agreed. There was an awkward silence before Mike spoke again. "I...I wish you were here with me, Elke," he said. "I miss you."

"Oh, and I miss you, Mike. I miss you terribly."

"We'll see each other soon," Mike assured her. "And I'll call you again tomorrow night."

"I will wait for your call," Elke said softly.

"All right, Elke. Goodbye."

After he hung up, Mike relaxed on his bed and looked up at the ceiling. He smiled. Well, he thought, at least the day ended on a good note. Was he falling in love with Elke? Probably. He shook his head. She was a German. He disliked Germans. And Germans had mistreated his wife horribly. But with it all, he was falling in love with Elke. Go figure that, will you!

CHAPTER FOURTEEN

The next morning, Mike visited the Hotel Montpensier, which was located on the Quai Voltaire, bordering the left bank of the Seine, and in view of the Louvre.

Employing basically the same cover story he had used with the concierge at the Albergo Dante in Rome, Mike had been able to learn that Behrens had been registered at the Montpensier from July 29 through August 4. This definitely put him in the city at the time the Paris letter had been mailed to Kaufman, the postmark having been August 2.

Mike also inquired about rental typewriters, learned the hotel had one, and tested it. As he suspected, the typed characters matched those in the letter sent to Kaufman.

Now, having left the Montpensier, Mike stood on the Quai Voltaire, mulling over the alternatives open to him. One of the glass topped Baton Mouche boats, carrying its load of tourists, glided up the nearby Seine. But Mike hardly noticed it, as he tried to plan his next actions.

What he had just learned at the Montpensier, Mike reasoned, seemed a further definite and solid link in the growing chain of circumstantial evidence against Behrens. Increasingly, it looked as if he was the German who had been sending Kaufman the threatening letters.

It seemed to Mike that his next step should be a trip to Milan and Florence. It was necessary to determine if Behrens had also been in those places at times coinciding with the postmarks on the letters. And he had to see if the hotels had typewriters, and if they had been used to write the letters.

Then, if things proved out as he suspected they would, he'd turn over this information to Craig, who would transmit it to the State Department in Washington. The State Department probably would then get in contact with the Italian and German governments, and arrange for Otto Behrens to be detained and conveniently put away for a while.

And that's the least that should happen to the bastard, Mike thought angrily. He deserves a lot worse than that, for the things he's been doing to Kaufman now, and for what he did to the Jews and other prisoners at Dachau.

I sure wish I could nail him personally, Mike thought to himself. He would have liked nothing better than to have returned to Rome and arrested Behrens, confronting him with the chain of evidence he had built up. But this, he knew, was impossible. Craig had been very strong in his warning against taking any unilateral action. Too much was at stake. Too much politics was involved, straight from Bonn, to Rome and Paris, and up to the White House in Washington.

Mike sighed as his thoughts now turned to Rabbi Dov Levin. There's the real victim of all of this, Mike thought, as he recalled the rabbi, shattered and withdrawn in his tiny apartment in Montmartre. To hell with all the politics that are involved. There's the real victim!

In anger mixed with frustration, Mike slammed his fist into his palm. He had been so sure that Behrens and the diary writer were one and the same! The phrase in the letters, and the phrase in the diary, were almost so exactly alike in wording. And that was too damn much of a coincidence to be passed over! There had to be a link between the two, and Mike had hoped the rabbi could provide it, could tender the knowledge that would definitely identify Behrens as the officer who had written the diary at Dachau.

But that was now an empty hope, Mike realized. His visit with Rabbi Levin had convinced him that the man's mind was almost totally gone. Any lucid memories probably were lost forever.

Mike shook his head as he recalled again the pitiful withdrawal of the man, when their conversation of last evening had become too painful. Mike thought about it, and then he made a decision. Milan and Florence could wait until tomorrow. He wanted to pay one more visit to Rabbi Levin. Not to ask him any more questions, but to try and bring him a little comfort.

Perhaps he might even take the old man out for the afternoon, give him a good meal and outfit him in some new clothing. Hell.

He deserved at least that much!

....

The noontime Paris traffic was a slow moving barrier to Mike's taxi. The cab passed easily enough over the Seine and through the Place de la Concorde, but its progress slowed considerably as it approached the heavy traffic of the Boulevard Haussmann, and moved into the small streets beyond. Consequently, it took Mike a half hour to reach Rabbi Levin's dwelling in Montmartre. It was 12:30 by that time, and Mike decided he definitely would invite the rabbi out for lunch, if the man was up to it.

Mike went into the building and started climbing the stairs. Even in midday, the inside of the building was dark, like a shadowy scene suspended in history. Anxious to reach the rabbi's apartment, Mike took the stairs two at a time.

He had just rounded the landing on the second floor, when he became aware of being watched. Mike stopped, and looked up the staircase. A man was standing there. A small man, dressed in a gray suit and hat.

The man seemed startled to see Mike. He remained motionless for an instant, his eyes darting about. Then, he started down the steps, limping slightly.

Mike moved aside to let him pass. There was something familiar in the man's appearance, but he couldn't place him. And as the man disappeared down the stairs toward the next landing, Mike shrugged and started up again toward the rabbi's apartment.

He reached the top floor and knocked on the door of apartment 3-B. No answer. Mike knocked again. Still no answer. Just as he had last time, Mike decided to try the door.

He turned the knob, pushed the door inward, and entered the room. Instinctively, he looked toward the window, the place where he had seen the rabbi standing when he came into the apartment last night. But the rabbi wasn't there.

Mike looked about the tiny room, and in the corner, he saw the rabbi. The man was lying on his cot, with his face to the wall. Mike hesitated, uncertain if he should awaken the rabbi. Perhaps it would be better to come back later, he thought. Only, he'd be leaving for Milan later.

Mike decided he'd wake the rabbi up. The man could always go back to sleep again. But it wasn't every day that the rabbi could have a full and substantial meal, and be given a new wardrobe.

Mike walked over to the cot, put his hand on the rabbi's shoulder and gently shook him. "Rabbi Levin," he called. "Wake up, Rabbi."

There was no response. And suddenly, something about the limpness of the rabbi's body made Mike suspicious. He bent forward, to look at the rabbi's face. It stared back at him, the eyes bulging and sightless, the tongue protruding from the mouth, contorted and twisted in its death throes. The rabbi was dead of strangulation.

The anger and bitterness swept through Mike, flowed to his eyes and smarted them with tears. For the man to have suffered so much, and now to have come to an ending like this. God damn it! What a way for him to die! And why?

Then, through his anger, Mike began to channel his thoughts back into a logical pattern. And he remembered the little gray man he had passed on the staircase. Now he knew why the man had seemed familiar to him. He fitted the description perfectly! The description the concierge had given at the Albergo Dante in Rome. Of the man who had visited Behrens. Yes. It was the same man who had called on Behrens!

Mike felt the rabbi's face. It was still warm. He must have been dead only a few minutes. Killed by the little gray man.

Mike ran from the apartment, down the stairs and out onto the street. He looked up and down both sides. Nothing. The man had disappeared.

CHAPTER FIFTEEN

Mike had made up his mind by the time he returned to his hotel. To hell with Florence and Milan. He was going back to Rome. To find the little gray man, whom, he was sure, was tied up with Behrens.

It all seemed to fit. Why else would the little gray man kill the rabbi? Because Behrens feared the rabbi would tell Mike something. And what could that be? All about Dachau, of course, and the identification of Behrens and the diary writer.

Brother, have I been stupid, Mike thought to himself. All this time he had been checking on Behrens, he had assumed the latter didn't know anything about it. But obviously, he did know exactly what Mike had been doing. Probably by having the little gray man follow him. And when Behrens found out that Mike had traced Rabbi Levin, and was seeing him, he gave the little gray man orders to kill the rabbi. To keep him quiet.

And the pity of the whole damn thing is that the rabbi couldn't tell me anything, anyway, Mike thought angrily to himself.

Back in Rome, he'd track down the little gray man, and through him, get to Behrens.

And Craig? Well, Craig would just have to be kept in the dark for a while. Mike felt certain he could do so for a couple of days, anyway. He'd call his chief from Rome, and somehow convince him that there was reason enough to be in Rome at that point, rather than in Florence and Milan, checking out Behrens' presence in the hotels in those cities.

Mike recalled Craig's warnings about avoiding any confrontations with Behrens. But God damn it. That poor Rabbi Levin. There had to be an accounting for his death. A reason for all of his sufferings. And Mike was determined to make that accounting come about, by proving that Behrens was behind everything. That it was Behrens who was torturing Kaufman with his letters. And that it was Behrens who also was the rabbi's killer. This time, Behrens had to be stopped. His identity at Dachau had to be uncovered, so that he could be made to pay for his crimes. Then, and only then, would there be a reason, a logical reason for Rabbi Levin's death.

The telephone rang. Before coming up to his room, Mike had asked the concierge to place a call to Elke in Frankfurt. He assumed this was it. He picked up the receiver.

"Mike? Is that you?" Elke asked.

"Yes. It's me," he answered dully.

"What's the matter? You sound so depressed. What is it?"

"The rabbi was murdered this afternoon."

"Oh my God. Are…are you sure it was…murder?"

"As sure as I'm talking to you. He was strangled."

"Are you all right?" Elke asked urgently.

"I'm okay," Mike answered brusquely. Then he apologized. "I'm sorry. I didn't mean to snap at you."

"It is all right," Elke reassured him. "I can imagine how you feel."

"I feel rotten. That's how I feel. Such a senseless killing. Done to keep the rabbi from telling me anything. And you know what? His mind was so far gone, that he couldn't possibly have told me anything. He was just a broken old man, living out his days, and he was killed."

"Was it Behrens, do you think?"

"I'm pretty sure he was responsible for it, though the actual killing was done by one of his people."

"Who?"

"I don't know his name. He's a short guy, dressed in all gray. And he limps in his left leg. He was coming down the stairs when I was going up to the Rabbi's apartment. I wouldn't even have suspected him. Only his description tallies with the one the concierge gave me at Behrens' hotel in Rome. The description of a man who used to visit Behrens."

"Did you say he was a short man? Dressed in gray? And he limps?"

"Yes."

"Mike!" Elke said urgently. "That man followed you on the

airplane in Frankfurt!"

"Are you sure?"

"As sure as I can be without seeing him again. After you had left me, and had started to board, he ran past me, toward the boarding gate," Elke explained.

Mike nodded thoughtfully. "It all begins to fit..."

"What do you mean?"

"Well, I figure Behrens must have heard, in Rome, that I was checking up on him. And so he got his little gray man to start trailing me. He followed me to Frankfurt, and then to Paris. Here, he saw me visit the rabbi. He checked with Behrens – that would explain the overnight delay – and Behrens must have told him to get rid of the rabbi. Behrens wanted the rabbi dead, because he was afraid the rabbi could identify him as the diary writer. Yes. It all fits!"

"Mike, I am frightened for you," Elke said strongly. "If Behrens had his agent kill the rabbi, then he may try to kill you, too."

"Don't worry," Mike reassured her.

"No, Mike. Listen," Elke said. "You are in danger. Please go to the police and tell them what you know. Please!"

"I can't"

"Why not?" she cried. "Because of your State Department and its plans? They are not important to me. But you are!"

"It's not only that," Mike answered. "Don't you see? I'm in this too deeply, now. Too deeply committed to it. Please try to understand. I've got to get Behrens and the little gray man. I've got to!"

"Mike, nothing will bring back the rabbi, now…"

"No, but at least I can give him the dignity of his death having had some meaning. Some reason."

"Oh, Mike…" Elke's voice trailed off in frustration.

"You've got to get hold of yourself, and stop worrying," Mike told her. "You've got to. Please. Promise me that, will you?"

"I…I will try."

"Good. That's my girl."

"What will you do now, Mike?"

"In the morning, I'm going back to Rome."

"To confront Behrens? Can you?"

"Not with any real accusations, of course. My orders say I can't do that. And even if I could, it would be a foolish thing to try at this point. The evidence isn't strong enough."

"Then, what will you do with him?"

"Oh, just play a little bit of cat and mouse."

"I…I am sorry," Elke faltered. "I do not know what this means. This…cat and mouse playing…?"

"It means I'm going to let him know what I know, but in a roundabout way. So that he's forced to make another move. And it also means letting him know about the little gray man, and that I know the two of them are connected. That ought to stir things up a bit!"

CHAPTER SIXTEEN

Mike arrived at Fiumicino Airport in Rome shortly after 1 PM the next day. But between customs and the 1 ½ hours needed to travel from the airport into town, it was well after 3:00 before he checked into his hotel.

Once in his room, he hopefully placed a call to the Albergo Dante, and without identifying himself, asked for Behrens. But just as he expected, the operator told him that Behrens no longer was a resident, and had left no forwarding address.

Finding Behrens was an important next step in the investigation, and Mike toyed momentarily with the idea of asking the Rome police for help.

But he rejected the notion, afraid that direct police action at this point would blow things up out of control, and take the matter too greatly out of his hands.

Of course, Mike thought to himself, Behrens probably isn't even hiding out at all. With the rabbi dead, he probably feels entirely safe.

Mike considered this possibility. It would be easy enough to check it out, he decided, and grabbing his hat, he hurried from the room.

....

"Ah, Signor Taylor," the Director of the Art Dealers Association greeted Mike a short while later. "What can I do for you?"

They were in Veranti's office. Mike had gone there from his hotel.

"Is this visit also about Signor Behrens?" Veranti asked.

"Yes, it is. I'm still working on the same investigation."

"And what is it I can do for you, now?" Veranti offered.

"Have you seen Behrens in Rome, recently? Or do you know where he might be living? I went to the Albergo Dante, but he had checked out."

"Oh? Well, I will inquire right now, as to whether we have a new address for him." He pushed the button on his intercom and spoke to the secretary in Italian, waited a moment until she answered, and then looked over at Mike. "No. I am sorry, Signor Taylor. The Albergo Dante was the last address we had for Signor Behrens."

"I see," Mike said, disappointed.

"But that is not to say that I have not seen Signor Behrens in recent days. I believe I saw him attending a gallery opening just the night before last."

"Here in Rome?" Mike asked hopefully.

"Yes." The Director pursed his lips thoughtfully. "And you know, I may see him tonight."

"How's that? Another gallery opening?"

"Yes. La Galleria de Montazi. A major opening which almost everyone will be attending. No doubt Signor Behrens will be there, too."

"Signor Veranti, do you think you might get me an invitation to the opening?" Mike asked. "I'd like very much to see Behrens."

"I am sure it can be arranged."

"And one more favor. Could you introduce us? That is, without Behrens really knowing who I am?" Mike was aware that Behrens did know who he was. And what he was doing. But Mike didn't want the Director to know this. And he also wanted to keep Behrens guessing as much as possible, keep him off balance. Being formally introduced in this way might help to do so, Mike felt.

"I would be happy to do whatever I can," Signor Veranti assured Mike. "My secretary will send an admission ticket to your hotel later this afternoon. I plan to be at the opening between 6:00 and 8:00. If you will come between those hours, I will look for you."

"Thank you, Signor Veranti," Mike said as he rose, shook the Director's hand, and walked to the door. Then, he turned.

"One more point, Signor Veranti. Do you know of a business associate of Behrens? I don't have his name. But he's a short fellow. Perhaps 5 feet 6 inches. Usually dressed in gray. And limps in his left leg."

The Director thought for a moment, then shook his head. "No. I do not recall seeing any such business associate of Signor Behrens. It does not sound like anyone that I know…"

Mike nodded. "Thank you. See you tonight, at the opening."

CHAPTER SEVENTEEN

La Galleria de Montazi, like most of the other major art galleries in Rome, was located on the Via di Babuino, and Mike had no trouble finding it. He arrived there at 7:00, figuring that Signor Veranti definitely would be in the gallery by that time.

But even though Signor Veranti probably was in attendance, so were at least 300 other persons. Mike couldn't see Veranti anywhere.

He decided to work his way over to the bar, get a drink, and then find a vantage point from which to look for Veranti. With considerable maneuvering and pushing, he reached his destination and obtained his drink. Then, he moved out of the mainstream to an area near the side of the bar and began scanning the crowd.

He was interrupted by a hand placed on his right arm. Mike turned to see who it was, and when he did, he was unable to suppress his surprise. The man, unmistakable from the broken nose, the thinning gray and dirty brown hair, and his other features, was Otto Behrens!

Behrens was looking at him intently, and Mike saw a flicker of a satisfied smile on the other man's mouth. Mike felt like kicking himself! Behrens had surprised him. Had caught him off guard. And it was obvious that Behrens knew it.

"I believe you have been making some inquiries about me, Mr. Taylor," Behrens said coldly, his dark eyes trained closely to Mike's face. "Is there something you are looking for?"

Mike took a few seconds to regain his composure, and to examine his adversary. In planning this meeting, Mike had decided it would be necessary to use a cover story when talking with Behrens. He knew that Behrens wouldn't really believe him. But that didn't matter. Mike felt that just so long as he didn't actually confront Behrens with anything resembling the true nature of his investigation, he would be staying within the restrictions outlined by Craig. And then, too, Mike hoped that his cover story might serve to draw Behrens out, so he could determine just how much the German really knew about the extent of his investigation.

Mike finally spoke. "Yes, as a matter of fact, I was looking for you," Mike said, launching into his cover story. "I'm with the U.S Immigration Service, you see…"

Behrens nodded curtly. "But of what interest can I possibly be to you? I am not applying for entry into the United States." Behrens' voice was controlled, the words carefully selected. And Mike sensed that Behrens was using their encounter in much the same way that he had intended to use it.

That is, as a testing ground for determining how much was

known.

"We're aware you're not applying for entry, Signor Behrens," Mike continued. "But your name came up during the course of an investigation we've been conducting on several persons of German extraction, who are applying for citizenship in the United States."

"I do not see how that is possible. I know no one in the United States. Of that I am certain."

"But your name did come up," Mike persisted.

"Who brought it up?" Behrens asked.

"A fellow named Jacob…Cramer." On purpose, Mike had used the first name of "Jacob", had paused, and had used a surname with the same first sound as "Kaufman." He hoped this ploy would bring about a reaction in Behrens. And though he couldn't be sure, he thought he did spot an involuntary nervous muscle tick on Behrens right temple, when he pronounced the name.

"I do not know any Jacob Cramer," Behrens answered quickly. "Nor anyone else in the United States."

Mike shrugged. "He gave your name as someone who could vouch for him. You see, he's having a difficult time accounting for his activities during the war. We of course don't want to grant him citizenship, if he was working in a concentration camp, or anything like that. In any event, when we began asking him about his whereabouts during the war, he was rather vague. Seemed to stick to some story that he was assigned to the Russian front the whole time. And he said you'd be able to verify it."

"Impossible," Behrens said calmly.

"Well, pretty much as I suspected," Mike said amiably. He leaned forward and spoke in a confidential voice. "You know, so many of these Germans who were involved in the concentration camp atrocities are trying to blot out the facts about what they were doing during the war. And this Cramer fellow is probably one of them." Mike stared intently at Behrens.

"I am sure I do not know," the other man answered, his voice flat and emotionless.

"By the way," Mike continued, "If you don't mind my asking, where did you spend the war?" He laughed in a friendly manner. "Now, you weren't assigned to any concentration camp, were you? Something like Auschwitz? Or Belsen? Or Dachau?"

"Of course not," Behrens answered casually. "I served in Africa and Italy. I never saw a concentration camp. During, or after, the war."

Mike shook his head. "Pretty rugged in Africa, I imagine."

"It was difficult," Behrens responded flatly.

"But, at least you were spared a close look at the atrocities some of your fellow Germans did perform on the Jews in the concentration camps." Mike sighed. "Pretty bad stuff. Killing everyone. I understand no one was spared. Even the spiritual leaders. Why, they even gassed the rabbis, same as everyone else. You might think the rabbis would have at least been spared. You know. Clergy, women and children being left alone? That kind of approach? But it wasn't the case."

"Now that you have learned that I do not know this…what was his name? This Jacob Cramer, will your investigation here be ending?" Behrens asked.

Mike knew the question was an important one to Behrens. He sensed Behrens was asking it, in order to try and gauge how much more he, Mike, planned to push the investigation. Mike looked intently at Behrens as he gave his answer.

"Hard to tell if and when it'll be ending. Problem is, I've got to check out some more facts that Cramer gave us. Or at least, they're supposed to be facts." Mike shook his head. "The more I get into it, the less truth I see in it. But, anyway, I might want the opportunity of speaking with you again, if you're agreeable. And by the way, where are you staying in Rome? Mind telling me?"

Behrens hesitated. "It is no secret," he finally said. "I am at the Excelsior."

Mike whistled. "Quite a switch from the Albergo Dante." He smiled at Behrens. "Things must be going well in the art business."

"I do not see why I should talk with you again, Mr. Taylor," Behrens said abruptly. "And I would deem it most inconvenient if you were to continue asking questions about me. I have my business interests to protect, of course."

"Of course," Mike agreed cheerfully. "And I have my job to do, as I'm sure you understand." He was purposely egging Behrens on, trying to get the man to commit some indiscretion. Anything that would break through the calm façade. But Behrens wouldn't rise to the bait.

"If you will excuse me, Mr. Taylor…"

Behrens walked away, without waiting for an answer from Mike. Mike looked after him. The meeting, he concluded to himself, had been pretty much of a standoff. He had learned nothing more from Behrens. And the latter probably didn't know any more, either.

Reluctantly, Mike concluded that he'd have to pay a visit the next morning to the Rome police. He wanted to try and get a line on the little gray man he had seen in the rabbi's apartment building. Perhaps they could help him. He imagined he could keep the police from getting too suspicious, by using the same cover story with them, as he had with Behrens. That is, that he was investigating the backgrounds of persons who had applied for U.S. citizenship. He finished his drink and began pushing his way toward the exit.

CHAPTER EIGHTEEN

Impatiently, Elke again looked at her watch. It was 8:15 PM. She rose, walked to one of the windows in the lobby of the hotel, and looked out. Still no sign of Mike. She returned to her seat, resigned to the fact that all she could do was wait. The concierge had told her Mike had gone out about 6:30, and had left word that he would be returning within a few hours.

Elke smiled as she envisioned Mike's surprise at seeing her in the lobby. He, of course, was not expecting her in Rome. And for that matter, she had not expected to be here, up until about 11:00 this past morning. That was when she had made the discovery in the diary. The important clue that she believed might now make things much clearer to Mike.

This morning, after checking her facts carefully, she had started to put a call in to Mike in Rome. But then she had changed her mind and decided to fly to him, instead.

She smiled, almost sheepishly, as she made the delightful admission to herself. Yes, she had flown to Mike in Rome, not only because of the new information she had to give him, even though it was possibly very important. The main reason she had come was, simply, that she was completely and utterly in love with Mike.

Elke sighed, deliciously lost in her thoughts. Love. It was a wonderful and exciting emotion. An all-encompassing magic that lifted her into a new plane of feeling, whenever she was with Mike.

"That's a fine thing. You come all the way from Frankfurt, to surprise me, I assume. And then you just sit there like a bump on a log. And I have to surprise you!"

"Oh!" Elke cried involuntarily, as she looked up to see Mike standing over her, grinning. "I did not see you come in."

"Obviously." Mike drew Elke to her feet, bent and kissed her, and then held her at arm's length. "And what brings you to Rome?" he smiled. "But before you answer, I want you to know that I am happier than hell to see you."

Elke raised her fingers to Mike's lips. "These bring me to Rome," she answered tenderly.

Mike laughed. "You can have more of them later," he promised her. "But I've got a feeling something else made you come down here, too." His face grew anxious. "Have you learned something new?"

"Yes, I have, Mike," Elke replied with excitement. "And it may be very important."

Mike led her to a couch in a quiet corner of the lobby and they sat down. "What is it?"

"Do you remember when you called me from Paris, and told

me about the little gray man you had seen leaving the building where the rabbi lived?"

"Yes."

"Well, as I told you then, I had seen the man myself. When he followed you on to the airplane in Frankfurt. But what I did not tell you was that I had sensed something familiar about him, then. It was only a vague feeling, however, and I did not pursue it. But when you described the man to me, on the telephone, I got the same feeling again. That there was something familiar about him. Only this time, the feeling was stronger."

"Probably because I had verbalized it. Spelled it out to you in words," Mike guessed.

"Possibly," Elke admitted. "But whatever it was, after we spoke, I felt more and more that the man, and especially the description of him, was familiar. That I had either seen him, or read something about him before."

"The diary!" Mike exploded, interrupting Elke's chain of explanation. "You had read about him somewhere in the diary!"

"Exactly!" Elke said. "That is just what it was!" She reached into the large handbag she was carrying and took out a brown filing envelope. From this, she removed the diary, and as Mike looked on, she opened it to a marked page.

"There," she said, as she gave Mike the diary, her finger pointing to a particular paragraph, "Read that."

Mike began reading the passage aloud, translating the German into English. "Today, I am afraid I took some undue advantage of my ever loyal Hans," the diary writer had recorded. "I and several of the other officers had a good deal of fun with one of the Jews. But it was at Hans' expense. It all began after we had some schnapps, following dinner. We decided we would have a Jew provide us with some entertainment. The question was, though, what sort of entertainment? And then someone came up with the idea. Simple, but enjoyable. We would bring in a young and agile Jew. And we would bring in Hans. And we would tell the Jew that he would be allowed to live, if he could avoid being caught by Hans, anywhere in our officers' quarters. The joker was, of course, that Hans, being lame in his left leg, and thus limping, would have a devil of a time catching the Jew."

Mike broke off from his reading, and excited, looked at Elke. "Hans and the little gray man! They both limped! They're the same person!"

Elke nodded in agreement. "But keep reading," she urged, "there is an additional description later on, that seems to make it even more certain an identification."

Mike resumed the narrative. "And it was a sight to behold! The Jew began scampering all about the quarters, with Hans in hot pursuit, bobbing up and down like a sewing machine needle, as he scurried after the Jew. I know of no way to describe Hans' movements, other than to say that he scurried. He didn't really run, because his limp prevented him from doing so. Yes, he scurried. That is the best word for it. Anyway, even though the Jew was young and agile, he was undernourished. And within a short time, the chase was over. Hans had caught the Jew, and we gave him a reward of permission to kill the youth, which Hans did, once he got him outside. Yes. It was much fun while it lasted. Of course, I made a point of apologizing to Hans afterwards. After all, we were in a sense taking advantage of his limp, in order to enjoy ourselves. But he accepted my apologies in the good grace he always has. And it is all well. He is quite an aide, that Hans of mine. This little man with the limp, and the scarred ear, who looked so unpromising when he first was assigned to me. He has developed into such a loyal aide, that every other officer envies me, I am sure. I can say unequivocally, that little Hans, limp, scar and all, would do anything for me. Anything."

Finished with the passage, Mike sat silently for a moment. Then he spoke, his words coming slowly and thoughtfully. "This really does seem to tie in the little gray man and Behrens, doesn't it?" he said, tapping the diary. "At least it makes it as certain as we possibly can be, without actually getting Behrens or the little gray man to admit anything."

"That was exactly what I felt when I read it," Elke agreed. "And..."

"Even the part about this Hans doing anything and everything for the diary writer," Mike interrupted her, "Even that fits. It goes a long way toward explaining how the little gray man would kill the rabbi, with no hesitation, on orders from Behrens."

"Yes, and..." Elke began, only to be interrupted again by Mike.

"But damn it," he said, "even as much as we feel we know now, we're still not any better off. I mean, we still haven't been able to trace either Behrens or this Hans, through the Army records of the people assigned to Dachau."

"But I have more on that, too," Elke said quickly, this time speaking very insistently, in order to prevent Mike from interrupting her once more. "If you will only give me an opportunity to finish a sentence!"

"I'm sorry, Elke," Mike apologized. "What is it?"

"Well, after I had read the passage, and came to the same conclusion as you now have, I began to think that perhaps there was another way to try and trace this aide, Hans. Perhaps, I thought, he might have been drafted into the Army with those disabilities. Perhaps he did not get those disabilities from being wounded in a battle, but had them before even being drafted. Many men were taken into the Army that way for limited duty. To do such things as being aides to officers, in fact. And if this were the case with Hans, then his army entrance medical records would show this."

"Same as in the American army," Mike said. "I remember, they were drafting guys with punctured eardrums, with glasses, stuff like that. They couldn't be expected to go into combat, and their medical records would say so. But they could be used for other duties."

"Exactly. In any event, I began going back over the medical records of every enlisted man who had served at Dachau, and who had the first name of Hans. Actually, it wasn't that difficult a task. There were only 47 enlisted men with that first name."

"And how many with a limp and ear lobe scar on their medical records?"

"Only one!" Elke announced triumphantly. "A Hans Zeitling, who limped in his left leg, and who was five feet and one half inches tall!"

"It sounds exactly like our man!" Mike cried.

"Wait! There is more," Elke continued. "Once I had Zeitling's record, it was possible to trace down where he had been drafted. Where he came from."

"What'd you find out?" Mike asked anxiously.

"He lived in Heidelburg, and that is where he was drafted from. So I called there, and spoke with the former head of the draft board. He remembered Zeitling, because the man had persisted in trying to enlist, despite his limp. And so finally, they had taken him."

"Does he know Zeitling now?"

"No. He said as far as he knows, Zeitling never came back to Heidelburg after the war."

"Damn!" Mike muttered.

"But it is not all that unfavorable," Elke added. "You see, the draft board chairman also told me that Zeitling's mother was still living, though she is an old woman. She resides in Heidelburg. And he believes, too, that she is the only family Zeitling has."

"So she might know his whereabouts! Maybe he's written to

her," Mike said hopefully.

"That is what I thought."

"And maybe, too," Mike continued, "she can tell us something more about the officer her son served as an aide." Mike snapped his fingers. "Hey! Wait a minute. I just thought of something else. Once you had Zeitling's medical record, weren't you able to check the duty rosters? And see what Zeitling's duties were? To make sure definitely he was the one who was an aide to an officer?"

Elke shook her head. "I attempted to do that." She paused meaningfully. "But there was no trace of Hans Zeitling in the duty roster records."

"Uh huh." Mike nodded thoughtfully. "That omission might be just as important as if his records had been in there. Hell! He and the officer were planning to go into hiding when the war ended, by changing their identities. So, they probably destroyed whatever records they could find about themselves in the Dachau files. Doesn't that make sense to you?"

"Yes," Elke agreed.

"It looks to me like our best bet, next, is to try and trace Zeitling's present location, through his mother in Heidelburg. And hopefully, too, she can give us the name of the officer to whom her son was an aide. Then we'll be able to trace the officer, too. And I'll bet both traces come right back here to Rome. To Behrens and his little gray friend!"

"If you are going to Heidelburg, I am going with you," Elke said.

"But," Mike protested, "you've gotten too involved in this thing already." He took her hands in his. "Look, I won't kid you. This investigation is getting more dangerous by the minute. They killed the rabbi, because they thought he knew too much. And they'll kill again, if they have to."

"But that applies as much to you as it does to me," Elke said. "If any person is in danger, it is you."

"That may be," Mike admitted. "But it's my job. And I can take care of myself." He cupped her face in his hand. "It's different with you, Elke. I don't want anything to happen to you."

Elke shook Mike's hand away from her face and looked steadily at him as she spoke. "There are many reason why I must come with you," she told him. "One is that I love you.
And I do not want to be away from you in this danger. But there is something else, too. I must see this through. Perhaps it is my feeling of guilt on behalf of my fellow Germans. Call it anything you like. But I feel I, as a German, owe it to the world, to see this through to the end. To do what I can to expose such awful beasts as Behrens and his Hans. I must! So please do not deny it to me!"

Mike realized that he could not convince Elke. He shrugged in surrender. "All right, you lovable nut," he said with deep feeling. "We'll go to Heidelburg together." He looked at his watch. "But not until tomorrow. Tonight, let's have a helluva dinner! Agreed?"

"Agreed," she smiled gratefully at him.

CHAPTER NINETEEN

Before they went to dinner, Mike put the Dachau diary back in its file envelope and deposited it in the hotel safe. At the same time, he told the concierge to book airplane reservations to Heidelburg for the next morning. Then, after they had both freshened up, Mike and Elke went out to dinner.

By the time they arrived at the restaurant, a small, plain trattoria in Trastevere, the old section of Rome, it was after 9:00. Mike had first become acquainted with the place years before. He had eaten there often during his stays in Rome, and the owner recognized him. They were treated to a multi-course dinner that belied the simple surroundings.

For the next few hours, Elke and Mike acted as newly discovered lovers have always acted, their sense of enjoyment of everything sharpened and finely honed. All thoughts of Behrens, Hans Zeitling, Dachau, the rabbi, Jacob Kaufman, were banished by the intimate glow of their romance.

Thus, the time passed, until, coming out of their reverie, they realized they were the last people in the trattoria, and that the indulgent owner was catching catnaps at his seat behind the cash drawer. It was 2:30 in the morning.

Smiling self-consciously, they rose. Mike paid the check, leaving a lavish tip behind, and they left the trattoria. The Rome night air was unusually cool for early October, and Elke sought shelter against it in the fold of Mike's arm. They began walking down the narrow street which eventually would lead them to the Viale di Trastevere. The street was deserted and quiet, and only off in the distance could they hear the more active sounds of the Viale di Trastevere.

Elke sighed contentedly, and Mike looked at her. "Happy?" he asked.

She nodded. "Very." Then she patted her stomach and grinned. "And full, too. That was a most wonderful dinner."

Mike laughed. "Just some good old fashioned Italian cooking. He has quite a memory, that Bernardo. I haven't been there in at least 7 or 8 years, and he remembered me right away."

Elke yawned. "I am feeling so wonderfully tired. I could sleep now, for days and days."

"I'm afraid that's not going to be possible," Mike said, looking at his watch, as they paused in the dim glow of one of the few lights that tried to illuminate the street. "Our plane takes off at 10:30, so we'll have to leave for the airport by 8:30. And that means getting up by at least 7:30. And that, My Dear, is only five hours from now."

"Beast," Elke muttered teasingly. "I am in love with a beast."

Mike leaned to kiss her. Their lips met and held, and at first, the loud noise that Mike heard didn't have any significance to him. It was only when the sound was repeated, that Mike realized someone was shooting at them.

Mike yanked Elke out of the glow of the street lamp, and half carried, half dragged her into the dark protection of a nearby doorway. Shielding Elke behind him, he reached under his suit coat and drew out his weapon. Then he peered cautiously into the street.

It seemed as deserted as before. Mike scanned both sides of the street, seeking some movement in the darkness. But he saw nothing.

He waited for a minute or so. Still no movement. Finally, Mike decided that whoever had been shooting at them, had slipped away when he and Elke scrambled into the doorway.

He put his weapon back into its shoulder holster and turned to Elke. She collapsed into his arms, trying hard to keep the sobs under her breath.

"Oh, Mike! Mike!" she cried.

Mike stroked her arm. "It's all right now, Elke," he assured her. "He's gone. It's all right now."

Elke fought to control herself, and finally did. She took a handkerchief from her pocketbook and blew her nose. Then, she breathed deeply. "I am sorry, Mike", she said resolutely.

"I am sorry I fell to pieces like that. I am all right now. I assure you, I am all right."

Mike looked intently at her, and she smiled back reassuringly. "Please, Mike," she said, "I am all right now. I really am."

"Okay, Elke," Mike said soothingly. "I believe you." Cautiously, he looked out onto the street. Then he grasped Elke by the arm. "Come on. Let's get back to the hotel."

"I did not know you carried a gun," Elke said a short time later, as they sat in their room at the hotel. They had reached the place with no further incident.

"I don't always carry one," Mike told her. "But I had orders to do so on this investigation."

"Who do you think shot at us, Mike?" Elke asked anxiously. "Do you think it was Behrens? Or the little gray man, Zeitling?"

Mike shrugged. "It could have been either one. I think it was more likely the little gray man, Zeitling, if that's his name. But he would have been acting on Behrens' orders, just like he did when he killed the rabbi in Paris."

"We are still going to Heidelburg tomorrow, though, Mike. Aren't we?" Elke asked, the determination clear in her voice. "This shooting will not stop us, will it?"

Mike grinned at her, in admiration. "You really are something, you know that? Back there, in the street, you were damn near hysterical. And now," he shook his head wonderingly, "and now, you're like a tigress who's lair has been threatened."

"I admit that I was terribly frightened when it happened," Elke answered. "And I still am." She looked intently at Mike. "But we must go on! We must. We cannot allow this to stop us!"

"I don't have any intention of letting it stop us," Mike answered. He rose and paced about the room. "You know," he said, "I must have done a better job on Behrens than I thought."

"What do you mean?"

"Well, when he and I met at that gallery opening this evening, I wanted to scare him. To try and provoke him into some indiscretion. But after our meeting, I concluded it was a standoff. That I really hadn't succeeded in accomplishing much of anything. But, I guess I was wrong."

"You mean, the reason he, or his man Zeitling, shot at us tonight, was because Behrens felt you knew too much?"

"Something like that." Mike sat down next to her. "And Elke," he said with satisfaction, "It also shows that we must be on the right track. There must be something definite to all of our thinking about Behrens being the Dachau diary writer. It's got to be. That's why the rabbi was murdered. And that's why we were shot at tonight!"

Elke shook her head. "This is all quite a change from the original purpose of your investigation, isn't it? I mean, you originally started out only to find the person who was writing threatening letters to Jacob Kaufman. And look where it has led. To the trail of a man we believe to be a Nazi war criminal. A man we think has been hiding out, ever since the end of the war."

Mike nodded. "That's what it looks like. More and more. And tomorrow in Heidelburg, here's hoping we get even closer to the truth."

CHAPTER TWENTY

At that same time, in an apartment in another part of Rome, two men were talking. Only one was in the apartment, however, the conversation being conducted over the telephone.

The man in the apartment was listening intently as the person at the other end of the line spoke. As he listened, the man paced about nervously, taking care to keep the long telephone cord from getting in the way of his lame left leg. His head bobbed up and down, seemingly in agreement with what the other person was saying.

He finally spoke "Yes. Yes. I am aware of that, of course." His tone was obedient, and his accent was German. "And I am most sorry that it turned out that way tonight. I was so sure I could get them. I am sorry."

Again, he listened obediently, his short, slight body sagging a bit, his head nodding in agreement. "Well," he said, "Their airplane departs for Heidelburg at 10:30 in the morning." Another pause, then, "Yes, I am sure of that. I wish, too, that it were possible for me to follow them to Heidelburg. But you are quite right. It would be too dangerous."

He listened again. "Yes, I realize how important it is to obtain and destroy the diary. And I am trying to do so. I hope to have success in this endeavor shortly."

The man again went silent as the other party resumed speaking. After another considerable period, he nodded his head.

"Yes. I understand. And it will be done," he said. Then he lowered the telephone from his ear and placed it on its cradle.

For a moment, the little man stood motionless, his eyes fixed on the telephone. Then, he reached into his pocket, took out a handkerchief and wiped his sweaty forehead.

CHAPTER TWENTY-ONE

It was well into the afternoon of the next day, before Elke and Mike arrived in Heidelburg, got through customs and reached the city itself.

Once they entered the city limits, the taxi's progress was slowed considerably in the narrow streets that characterized the 12th century origins of Heidelburg. Finally, however, the vehicle pulled up before one of the small and immaculate apartment dwellings that was so typical of the city.

"Number 12 Strasse Kimmel," Mike said, as he spied the building's address. "This is it."

Mike paid the fare and helped Elke from the taxi. "Remember our cover story," he cautioned her as they walked toward the building.

Elke nodded, and they went inside. The building had only a few apartments, and they quickly located the name, "Zeitling," for apartment 1-A.

"I hope that she is at home," Elke said as they walked up the staircase to the first floor.

"We'll know quickly enough," Mike answered. They reached 1-A, and Mike knocked on the door.

"Just one moment, please," came an almost immediate response from within, in German. It was a woman's voice.

Slow footsteps approached the door. Then, a lock was unlatched and the door was opened slightly.

"Ja?" An elderly woman peered out at them.

"Mrs. Zeitling? Elke asked.

The woman nodded. "I am Mrs. Zeitling," she answered.

"May we come in and talk with you?" Elke asked. "I am with the German government. This gentleman is with the American government. And we would like to talk to you about your son, Hans."

The old woman's face took on a sudden expression of hope. "You have news of my son? You know where he is?" she asked eagerly.

"We have some news," Elke answered quickly. "But, may we come inside and talk with you?"

"Ja. Ja," Mrs. Zeitling said with excitement, opening the door and motioning them into the apartment. "Please. Tell me. Is he alive, my son? Is he well? After all these years, do you have news of him? It is a miracle, I tell you. It is a miracle!"

Elke looked at Mike, an expression of helplessness on her face. This wasn't as they had expected it to be. Neither of them had been prepared for this emotional outburst. They just hadn't taken it into consideration, so wrapped up were they in the investigation.

And they both suddenly realized the enormous cruelty they were bringing to bear on this woman, who obviously was now in the process of resurrecting hopes about her son. Hopes that had been buried long ago.

Hating himself for it, but realizing it was necessary, Mike picked up the conversation. He placed a soft but restraining hand on Mrs. Zeitling's arm. "Let me point out immediately, Mrs. Zeitling," Mike spoke in German, "that we do not at this moment know where your son is. But we are looking for him. And with your help, we may be able to find him." He felt like a louse, telling the woman these half-truths, but he knew it had to be done.

Mrs. Zeitling wrung her hands together and fought to control her emotions. "You must excuse me," she apologized. "What is wrong with me? Please. Sit down. Would you like some tea, perhaps?"

"No thank you, Mrs. Zeitling," Mike answered as he and Elke settled into a couch in the small living room. "We just want to talk with you."

Mrs. Zeitling sat down in a nearby chair. "Yes?" she said encouragingly.

Although he didn't really have to, Mike consulted his pad. He felt it would fit in better with his cover story, into which he now launched. "Your son is, Corporal Hans Zeitling, who served at Dachau?" he asked.

"Yes," Mrs. Zeitling answered eagerly. "But of course, I am sure my Hans had nothing to do with those awful things they say took place there. He was not that sort of boy. You must believe me. I am sure he was only doing his duty."

"Of course," Mike forced himself to agree. Now, he felt less badly about deluding Mrs. Zeitling as to the purpose of their visit. Her righteous denial about her son's wrongdoing was just the attitude he had come to hate among Germans. An attitude that rejected any responsibility for the acts of the Third Reich.

"And let me assure you," Mike continued, "that the purpose of our coming here, has nothing to do with the events at Dachau. The only thing we are interested in is helping you locate your son, Hans. You see, both the American and German governments have recently started a program to locate, once and for all, as many of the missing persons as possible, from the war. Both governments believe it is time for final and total peace and happiness to return to all the war torn homes and families. To people such as yourself. People who can't find their loved ones. And that's our only purpose in coming here today, Mrs. Zeitling. And hopefully, with your help, we'll be able to find Hans."

Mrs. Zeitling nodded. "And what can I do?"

"We have to ask you several questions. And as much information as you can give us, that will be the most helpful thing you can do. Agreeable with you?"

"Ja."

"Now. Have you seen your son, Hans, at all, since the end of the war?"

"No."

"When was the last time you heard from him? Was it after the end of the war?"

"No. I have not heard from Hans since before the war ended," Mrs. Zeitling said sadly. "Not for these 19 years."

"Did you hear from him, while he was stationed at Dachau?"

"Ja. Ja. He used to write to me." She sighed. "Not often. But you understand, he was very busy. He had much to do."

"What did he tell you he was doing at Dachau? What was his assignment there?" Mike asked hopefully. If Mrs. Zeitling confirmed that her son was an aide to an officer, then Mike knew this conversation might be the most important one he'd had, since first starting his investigation of Behrens.

"He had a very important position," Mrs. Zeitling said, with a mother's pride. "He was an aide to an officer. His personal aide," she emphasized.

That was it! Now they were really on the right track!

"Of course," Mrs. Zeitling continued proudly, "Hans was not able to write me too much of what his duties were. Very important, and very secret, you understand. But I could tell, from the little he was able to write, that my Hans was performing an important service."

"You must have been very proud of him," Elke encouraged Mrs. Zeitling.

"Yes. Of course," she answered.

Mike resumed his questioning. "And you say, he was a personal aide to an officer?"

"That is correct."

"Do you know the officer's name?" Mike asked, sensing Elke's tenseness beside him. They both knew that this was the key question, the entire reason for their flight from Rome to Heidelburg. "Did your son write you about who his officer was?"

Mrs. Zeitling shook her head. "My son never wrote me the name of his officer," she answered strongly. "I told you," she added with impatience, "my son's work was very secret. He could tell me only very little about it. And of course, he could not write me the name of his officer!"

Mike sighed. "That's too bad," he said, speaking half to Mrs. Zeitling and half to himself. "That's too bad."

"But nonetheless, I do have the officer's name," Mrs. Zeitling announced.

Mike looked sharply at the woman.

"Ja," Mrs. Zeitling continued. "It was in the newspaper article about Hans," she said proudly. "An article all about my son in the Heidelburg paper.

"Do you still have that article?" Mike asked quickly.

Mrs. Zeitling beamed. "Of course I have it. It was about my son, no?" She rose and walked to a small bookcase in a corner of the room. Stooping, she selected what appeared to be a scrapbook from one of the lower shelves. Then, she returned with it to her chair. With obvious familiarity, she leafed through the pages of the album and then handed the book to Elke, while pointing at one of the pages on which a yellowed newspaper clipping was pasted.

Elke began reading aloud. "Corporal Hans Zeitling, Number 12 Strasse Kimmel, is honorably serving the Fatherland's cause in his Army duty at his station in Dachau," the first paragraph of the article began.

Listening, Mike realized that the story was one of those typical, standardized news releases that all armies periodically send out to hometown newspapers, about the boys in service. In the American Army, this was the function of the Public Information Office, PIO. And Mike assumed a similar propaganda office had existed in the German Army, an office with the sole function of pumping out stories about the troops, in order to bolster the morale of the people at home.

Elke continued to read the short article aloud. "Corporal Zeitling is assigned as personal aide to Captain Max Schmidt, who reports that the Corporal is an outstanding soldier."

"What do you think of that," Mrs. Zeitling broke in proudly. "Right there. In the article. How good my Hans was."

Mike forced himself to nod agreeably at Mrs. Zeitling. Obviously, the words characterizing Hans Zeitling as an outstanding soldier were part of the standard phraseology that went into the hundreds of thousands of such news stories that were sent out continuously to the hometown newspapers. He looked at Elke. "Anything else to the story?"

"Just one more paragraph," she answered, resuming her reading. "It can be reported that Corporal Zeitling, from the time he first joined the Fuehrer's cause, has conducted himself in true soldierly fashion, and his family can be duly proud of him." Elke looked at Mike. "That is all," she told him.

Mike allowed himself a smile. They had it! They had the name of the officer. The diary writer! Captain Max Schmidt. Mike shook his head. It was ironic. Truly so. Schmidt had tried so hard to blot out his identity. Had tried to erase it by removing every record he could lay his hands on at Dachau. By even trying to burn his own diary. But now, over 19 years later, and through a stupid little thing like a propaganda announcement, he was uncovered. Captain Max Schmidt. And it would lead, Mike felt almost certain, right to Rome, and to Behrens!

But Mike wasn't finished with Mrs. Zeitling, yet. There were other things he hoped she'd be able to tell him, and he resumed his questioning.

"That certainly is a wonderful article about your Hans," he said to Mrs. Zeitling. "And now, tell me, did Hans ever describe his officer? Captain Max Schmidt? Did he ever tell you anything about him?"

Mrs. Zeitling furrowed her brow. "Sometimes, in his letters, he would say something. A little bit of something about the Captain, without giving his name, of course."

"What did he write?" Mike encouraged her.

"Well, one thing which impressed Hans was that his officer was a very cultured man. Very cultured. He mentioned this in his letters. How his captain was very cultured."

"What did he mean by that?" Mike asked.

"Oh, you know. Hans said his captain was cultured in the fine things. He read many books. And yes, I remember now. Hans said his captain was an authority on art, on painting."

"Mike!" Elke said involuntarily.

Mike nodded, and thought, it fits all the way. The description of Captain Schmidt, as an art authority, fit Behrens just perfectly.

Mike asked Mrs. Zeitling. "Anything else? Anything else that describes the Captain? Or, did Hans ever send you a picture of Captain Schmidt?"

"No. No picture."

"What about Hans? Do you have a picture of him?"

"Ja. He looked so wonderful in his uniform. Do you want to see it?"

"If we may…"

Mrs. Zeitling leaned across to Elke and flipped back a few pages in the album that Elke was still holding in her lap. "There," she said, pointing to a small snapshot. "There is a picture of Hans."

Both Elke and Mike leaned forward to look at the picture, and Mike felt Elke's body grow tense beside his. There was little chance of mistaking it. Although the man in the picture was only in his mid-20's, the similarities between he and the little gray man were conclusive. Hans Zeitling and the little gray man, definitely were one and the same!

Mike asked Mrs. Zeitling. "Would it be possible to take this picture with us? I'll return it shortly. After I've made a copy."

"You will be sure to return it?" Mrs. Zeitling asked, worried.

"Within a few days," Mike assured her.

"All right," Mrs. Zeitling agreed. She looked anxiously at Mike. "Do you think you will be able to find my son? To find my Hans? One day, I knew he was stationed at Dachau. And then the war ended. And I heard nothing more from him. Do you think you will be able to find him?"

"I hope so, Mrs. Zeitling," Mike answered her, but for reasons far different from hers. "I truly hope so."

"He was such a good son," Mrs. Zeitling said. "And a good soldier, too." She shook her head. "He wanted so much to be a soldier. And at first, they would not take him, because of his leg."

"What was wrong with his leg?" Mike asked, almost certain what the answer would be.

"He was lame in the left leg. Oh, not so badly so, mind you. But he did limp a little. And for that, they would not take him in the army, at first." Mrs. Zeitling looked proudly at Mike and Elke as she spoke. "But finally, they took him. And he was a good soldier. You read the article in the newspaper. My Hans was a good soldier!"

They left Mrs. Zeitling then, and once they were around the corner, out of sight of the building, Mike stopped and spoke to Elke.

"This looks like it Elke! It really looks like we're on the right track. There's no doubt about Hans Zeitling being the little gray man."

"And Captain Max Schmidt. We have his name at last! Our

diary writer," Elke added.

"And now we've got to track him down," Mike said. "Elke, can you call your headquarters in Frankfurt, and start a trace on Captain Max Schmidt?"

"Yes," Elke said. She looked around the street, then pulled at Mike's sleeve. "Come. There is an inn. It must have a telephone we can use for the call to Frankfurt."

CHAPTER TWENTY-TWO

Mike and Elke made almost immediate airplane connections to Rome, and were back in the city by mid-evening of the same day.

When they reached their hotel, the concierge had a message for Mike. Craig had called several times from New York, and had left word for Mike to return the call, regardless of the time.

Mike looked at his watch. It was 9:30 in Rome, making it 3:30 in the afternoon in New York. He instructed the concierge to put the telephone call through, to Craig's office.

Then they settled down to await the call, which came almost immediately.

"Taylor? Is that you?" Craig asked, true to his usual pattern of omitting all social preliminaries.

"Where the hell have you been? I've been trying to get you all over Europe, damn near. I figured you'd be somewhere in Milan or Florence."

"I was in Heidelburg today, Chief, and I turned up a lot of interesting things," Mike started to explain.

"Heidelburg? What do you think you have?
And unlimited arrangement with the expense account people at the Treasury Department?" Craig demanded. "But anyway," he continued, without waiting for an answer, and suddenly switching subjects, "the fact is, that you can forget about the whole investigation and come home."

"Forget about it!" Mike echoed in surprise. "What do you mean? I don't understand."

"I mean exactly what I said," Craig snapped. "Forget about the investigation!" Then, his tone softened considerably. "Mike, I'm sure you don't want to hear this. It's a crazy situation. And I don't like it any more than you do, this cutting off of something right in the middle. But there's nothing we can do about it. You'll have to drop the investigation."

"What happened?"

Craig sighed. "Nutty as it is, the investigation is being dropped at Jacob Kaufman's request. And the order to drop the investigation is just as definite, and just as highly placed in the Administration, as was the order to start it in the first place. In other words, it is over, with a capital 'O', and completely so."

"But why did Kaufman want it dropped? And especially now, when I think I've really got something definite. I didn't even tell you what I found in Heidelburg, Chief…"

"I don't want to know what you found," Craig cut him off again. "Kaufman has asked his connections at the State Department, and elsewhere, to drop the whole thing. And so we drop it."

"Did Kaufman give any reason?" Mike asked.

"A guy with connections like he has, doesn't have to. But he did give a reason, anyway. Remember his daughter? The one who's getting married soon?"

"Yes."

"Well, as you know, she wasn't supposed to know anything about all this. The letters, the investigation, it all was supposed to be kept secret from her, because of her earlier nervous breakdown."

"Did she hear something about the investigation?" Mike broke in. "Is that why Kaufman's calling it off?"

"Yes. Kaufman says she doesn't know too much. But she knows something is going on. And she's starting to get upset. And he says nothing can be allowed to continue on the investigation, if it will upset her."

"But this thing's gotten bigger than Kaufman! Or his daughter!" Mike protested.

"You're forgetting one thing," Craig reminded him. "It was Kaufman who requested this investigation in the first place. So, when he asks for it to be stopped, he gets a sympathetic ear. Hell! The State Department was never very happy about the whole thing, right from the beginning. It has the potential of being a real hot potato. And all along, State's been hoping the case would just go away and die a quiet death somewhere. Well, Kaufman's request for the investigation to stop, has given State what it was looking for. An out. And so it all ends. As of now. And you come on home."

Mike was about to accede, reluctantly, when a sudden impulse hit him. "Chief," he said to Craig, mustering up a casual voice, "I've got a favor to ask of you."

"What's that?"

"Well, instead of coming home right away, how about if I were to take my vacation time now, and stay in Europe? I've got three weeks coming to me. And this way, I'll be saving myself the air fare of a European vacation."

"You're not figuring on continuing this investigation on your own, are you, Taylor?" Craig asked suspiciously.

Mike decided to pull out all the stops. "Hell, no," he countered with as much sincerity as he could. "As a matter of fact, I'm thinking about something else, entirely. I wasn't going to tell anyone yet. But anyway, the fact is, I've met a girl here, Chief. And, well, I think this is for real. And I'd like to spend the next few weeks with her."

Mike couldn't help noticing Elke's puzzled, then pleased, then again puzzled expressions, as she tried to follow the meaning of his conversation with Craig. Mike put a cautioning finger to his lips, as Elke seemed about to say something.

There was a momentary pause at the other end of the line, as Craig thought over Mike's request. Mike kept silent, sensing that to say anything further would arouse Craig's suspicions.

Finally, Craig spoke. "Well, all right," he said hesitantly.

"You can have your three weeks. But god damn it," he warned, "if I find out that you're still on this investigation, you might as well not bother coming back. Understand?"

"I understand," Mike assured him.

After putting down the telephone, Mike turned to look at Elke. "The investigation is being called off," he said bitterly. "And just when we're getting so close!"

"Oh, Mike. I am so sorry," Elke told him.

"Damn!" Mike exploded. "Maybe they can call it off. But I'm not!"

"That is why you requested your vacation now? To continue the investigation?"

Mike took Elke's hand. "Elke, Dear. What I said to Craig on the telephone, about us, was the truth. Even if I didn't feel so strongly about getting Behrens, I would have asked Craig for the vacation time. So I could be with you for the next three weeks. That part of what I told him was entirely true."

"But you feel you must go on with the investigation, too?" Elke asked.

Mike nodded. "Yes. It'll have to be without Craig's knowledge, of course."

"And it is dangerous for your career, is it not? If he found out, it would ruin you," Elke said.

"That doesn't matter!" Mike answered quickly. "Look. Don't you see? What about that poor rabbi who died in Paris, because they thought he could tell me something? And he couldn't even do that, so what the hell did he have to die for? I've got to give him an answer. And what about whoever was taking pot shots at us last night?" He paused. "And what about the others? In Dachau and everywhere else? They've got to have answers. And not the kind Mrs. Zeitling has for her son, Hans. The kind of answer that claims Hans, and the others like him, had nothing to do with what went on at Dachau. That they were only doing their duty."

Elke put a restraining finger up to Mike's lips. "I am in love with an idealist," she said tenderly, smiling at him.

Mike returned her smile. "I'm afraid so," he admitted. "Sorry?"

"No," she answered strongly. "No. Never."

They looked at each other momentarily, and then Mike let go of Elke's hand and started pacing about the room, thinking.

"What happens now?" Elke asked. "Where do we go from here?"

"We go on with our investigation of Behrens, and his little gray man," Mike said grimly. "In other words, Captain Max Schmidt and Corporal Hans Zeitling. War criminals on the run. And murderers of a defenseless old man in Paris." He turned to look at Elke. "We've got three ways to go at it. And we'll use all of them."

"What are they?"

"First," Mike began, using his fingers to tick off the alternatives, "Let's remember that regardless of whatever letters Behrens has been writing to Jacob Kaufman, and even if that particular investigation is supposed to be called off, there's another big angle to all of this."

"You mean, about Behrens and Zeitling, or whatever he calls himself now, being escaped war criminals?"

"Exactly. So, even if we don't ever succeed in tying in Behrens with the letters to Kaufman, we can still nail Behrens and Zeitling just as solidly on the basis of their being war criminals. I'm sure the German government would like to know about them. So, we've got to prove that Behrens and the little gray man are Captain Max Schmidt and Corporal Hans Zeitling. And our starting point for that is already underway, namely the trace you've requested on Schmidt. How long do you figure it will take for it to come through?"

Elke shrugged. "It is difficult to say. A week. Ten days. Perhaps a bit longer. You see, Max Schmidt is a fairly common name in Germany."

"Well, at least we're on the way, in that part of your investigation," Mike commented. He held up a second finger. "And now for the second part. That is, to determine, in Florence and Milan, if Behrens was in those cities at the times the threatening letters were mailed to Kaufman. That's important, because it would complete the picture, since we've got the facts established about Rome and Paris. I'll have to go up to Milan and Florence, and check those cities out."

"Let me go," Elke interrupted.

"You?"

"Yes. I will go to Florence and Milan and check out the facts about Behrens and the hotels, and when he was in those cities."

Mike shook his head. "No. I can't let you do it. It's too dangerous."

"It is not," Elke countered. "Whatever danger there is, I am sure it will be directed toward you. I do not really represent any threat to anyone. After all, looked at in a practical sense, I am only a clerk in the German government. You are the one who is carrying out this investigation."

"I don't know..." Mike mused.

"And besides," Elke pushed her argument, "we must move quickly. Your supposed vacation is only for three weeks. And then you definitely must return to New York. So, we must learn everything before the three weeks are over. And then, too, how long do you think you will be able to keep word from getting back to Craig, in New York, about your continuing the investigation? So, it is necessary to do as much as possible in the least amount of time, and using all of our resources. And that," she concluded triumphantly, "means that I will go to Florence and Milan."

In spite of himself, Mike had to laugh. "Did anyone ever tell you, you would have made a hell of a lawyer?" He became serious again. "I still don't like it, Elke. Are you sure you'll be careful? You won't do anything foolish? You'll just get the facts at the hotels and then come right back to me?"

"Yes, Mike," Elke promised him. "And now, what is the third way you were talking about?"

"It's picking up the trail of Behrens and his little gray man, right here in Rome. For one thing, I want to trace back over Behrens' life in the city. When did he get here? What's he done since he's been here? Then, hopefully, when I get to the beginning of that story, it'll tie in directly with what the trace on Max Schmidt turns up. In other words, we'll have ourselves a direct link between the Max Schmidt of Dachau and the Otto Behrens of Rome. And that'll be just what the German government will need, to prosecute him as a war criminal"

Mike paused, thought, and then continued. "And finally, there's one more thing to be done."

"What?"

"I want to establish if Behrens was in Paris, too, at the time the rabbi was murdered. I know Zeitling was. But in both cases, I've got to get the details on paper."

Mike stopped his pacing and stood in front of Elke. "We've got a lot to do." He smiled at her. "Some vacation, huh?"

CHAPTER TWENTY-THREE

"Yes. Yes, I am certain. I followed them to the airport and watched Taylor put the girl on the airplane for Florence. Then, I followed Taylor to his hotel, before coming back here to telephone you."

The speaker was the little gray man, whom Mike and Elke had identified as Hans Zeitling. He was standing by the telephone in his apartment, his short body unconsciously drawn up to a position of near attention, as he listened to the voice at the other end of the line.

"I do not know exactly why she is going to Florence. But I would assume it is to do as Taylor has done in Rome and Paris. That is, to check on the hotels and to see if they coincide with the dates of the letters, and if the typewriters are the same." Another pause. "No. Taylor does not have passage to either Florence or Milan. And the girl's ticket is for continuation to Milan, after she stops in Florence. So, I assume Taylor is staying in Rome."

Zeitling nodded his head several times as the other person again spoke. Then he answered. "I do not know. It is impossible to tell whether the diary is still in the hotel safe, or with the girl."

He nodded again. "Yes, I know I must find out, and obtain the diary. Yes, I know. At all costs." Unconsciously, he had come rigidly to attention. "Yes, I will do it," he promised. "You can rest assured I will do it."

Zeitling lowered the telephone and stood immobile for a moment. Then he turned toward the window and looked out. Situated as it was on one of the many hills on the outskirts of Rome, Zeitling's apartment offered him an impressive view of a large part of the city. But he noticed little of the overall skyline. Instead, his eyes searched the city's landscape, as if seeking out the specific whereabouts of Mike Taylor in order to learn exactly what the American was doing at that moment. This American, who posed such a threat to them.

Finally, Zeitling sighed and allowed his body to relax. He glanced at his watch, then turned, and in his awkward, limping walk, hurried across the room. There was much to be done.

CHAPTER TWENTY-FOUR

Mike, too, was in a hurry at that same time. It had been a busy day. First, he had taken Elke to the airport, and seen her off to Florence, after again extracting her promise to be careful. Then, he had returned to Rome, and had called on Signor Veranti at the Art Dealers Association. His purpose in visiting Veranti had been to obtain the names of several art dealers who might be able to provide background information on Behrens.

As always, Signor Veranti had been most gracious. And after some careful thought, he had compiled a list of six art dealers whom he believed had dealings with Behrens and who might be able to provide Mike with the information he needed.

By the time Mike had finished meeting with Signor Veranti, it was almost 12:30. And knowing Rome, Mike realized it was useless to call on any of the art dealers until at least 4:00.

After waiting impatiently in his hotel room until 4:00 neared, Mike set out toward the Via di Babuino. All of the art dealers on the list were located there. With luck, Mike figured he could see all six before 7:30, closing time. Then, he'd be able to get back to the hotel in time for Elke's telephone call from Florence. She was supposed to call about 8:00 or 8:30, and let him know what she had found at the Albergo Aprile, the place Behrens stayed when he visited Florence.

The first name on Mike's list was a Signor Luigi Morabito. Signor Veranti had told Mike that Morabito was a moderately successful art dealer who had several transactions with Behrens. Veranti also had told Mike that Morabito was a garrulous man. The sort who liked to gossip, and hence, a good person for Mike to question.

Once in Morabito's gallery, Mike had sent in a note from Veranti. After a short wait, one of the sales clerks conducted Mike to an office in the rear of the gallery, where Signor Morabito, smiling, awaited him.

"Signor Taylor?" Morabito greeted him in English and with an outstretched hand.

"Yes," Mike answered. "And thank you for taking time to see me. I appreciate it."

"But of course," Morabito said, as he led Mike into his office, and guided him to a large couch, where they both sat down. "Signor Veranti said in his note that he would appreciate all courtesies to be extended to you. And I am only too glad to do so."

"Signor Veranti said that you might be able to give me some information about a certain, Otto Behrens," Mike said.

"Of course, your discretion would be appreciated as concerns anything we discuss here today…"

"Of course. Of course," Morabito hastily assured him. Mike could tell, though, that Morabito's assurances had little meaning. Veranti was right. Morabito appeared to be a talkative one.

"Is...is Signor Behrens in some difficulty?" Morabito asked Mike, hardly able to conceal the intensity of his interest.

"No," Mike assured him. "I just want some information."

"Well," Morabito smiled at him while opening his arms wide in a welcoming gesture, "what is it I can do for you?"

"You do know Signor Behrens, I take it?"

Morabito nodded vigorously. "Yes, I know him."

"Through business dealings with him?"

"That is correct."

"How long have you known Signor Behrens?"

Morabito thought for a moment, then shrugged. "For many years. Perhaps ten, or longer."

"You met him first in Rome? Perhaps ten or more years ago?"

"It might even be fifteen," Morabito reflected. Then he nodded at Mike. "But it was in Rome. Of this I am certain."

"How did you first meet him?" Mike asked.

"Through a business dealing. It involved my purchase from him of some minor paintings."

"Did you have many business dealings with him in the years after that?"

"Not many, but some."

"Did Signor Behrens ever talk about what he did, before he came to Rome?" Mike asked.

Morabito thought for a moment. "No. I do not recall that he spoke of much of anything, other than business. We were not, as you would say, good friends."

"Did he ever say anything at all about how he spent the war years? About his military service, or anything like that?"

Morabito shook his head. "Never."

Mike switched to another line of questioning. "Tell me this, Signor Morabito. Did Signor Behrens have any friends whom you know of? Any Germans, perhaps, who were often seen in his company?"

"I really do not know," Morabito answered. "You must understand. Signor Behrens and I merely had business dealings together."

"There is a particular person whom you might have seen in Behrens' company from time to time," Mike persisted. "Perhaps you'll recall him, if I describe him. He's a short man, about five feet six inches. Quite thin. And he has a limp in his left leg." Mike took out the picture of Hans Zeitling. "This is a picture of the man. From about 20 years ago. Does he look at all like anyone you've ever seen in Behrens' presence?"

Morabito examined the picture and then shook his head. "No. He does not look at all familiar to me."

He looked apologetically at Mike. "I am not of much aid, am I, Signor Taylor? I am very sorry."

"Well, let me ask you this, then. When was the last time you saw Behrens?"

"Ah, now I can answer you," Morabito said heartily. "That is an easy one. I last saw Signor Behrens several days ago. It was one evening last week. At a gallery opening."

"Have you had any business dealings with him lately?"

Morabito grew thoughtful. "You know, now that you bring it to my attention, I realize that I have not had any business dealings with Signor Behrens in several months. And that is most unusual."

"Why is it so unusual?" Mike asked, his interested heightened. "Is Behrens that active an art dealer? I had heard that he was a relatively unimportant person in the art world."

"You have heard correctly," Morabito agreed. "Behrens is not very important. He is a minor figure, at best. But he is active. Always trying. Always pushing his small, unimportant wares." Morabito shrugged, then continued, half aloud and musingly. "But he has not been active, at least with me, in recent months. And yet, I note that he is looking more and more prosperous. Now that I think about it, I wonder with whom he is dealing."

There was something familiar about Morabito's last remarks, Mike felt. And then he realized what it was.

Morabito's comments about Behrens' recent prosperity coincided with similar comments that had been made by Signore Veranti, and the concierge at Behrens' old hotel, the Albergo Dante. Mike's interest was aroused.

"Signor Morabito," he explained to the art dealer, "Some other people have commented to me about the fact that Signor Behrens seems to…to have more money now, than in the past. Or, at least, to be dressing better, and living in a better hotel. Tell me. Can you recall how long this has been going on? When was it that Signor Behrens first seemed to begin to look more prosperous?"

Morabito paused before replying. "It is several months," he said reflectively. "Of this I am sure. It is several months that he has been appearing so much more prosperous."

"Have you any idea where he's getting his money? I mean, if he's not dealing with you much anymore, do you know who he is dealing with? Or, if he had any particularly major transactions in recent months?"

Morabito shook his head. "I do not know with whom he has been dealing. But I do know he has been talking quite a bit about some business transactions."

"What's he been saying?"

"He has not been saying anything specific," Morabito explained to Mike. "There are no definite transaction that he has mentioned. But he…he has been making many…many vague remarks."

"Like what?"

"Oh…he has been saying that he soon will acquire an interest in an important art gallery."

"Do you have any idea what gallery that might be?"

Morabito shrugged. "Ah, Signor Taylor. I do not know. And I cannot even imagine it. He is such a minor person in our world. Why he would be in a position to acquire an interest in an important gallery, I do not know. But I do know that he has been speaking of this. Not only to me, but to others. And," Signore Morabito gestured, "It must be. After all, he is living rather well now, no? He looks much different from when I first met him."

This same theme, about Behrens' seemingly recent acquisition of money, and some pending major business association, reoccurred in each of the interviews Mike had with the other art dealers during the remainder of the afternoon.

All of the art dealers had first become acquainted with Behrens between 10 and 15 years ago, making it about 1950 to 1955. All had dealt with him on minor works of art. None knew anything of his background before 1950.

From the conversations, two facts seemed important to Mike. These were, Behrens' improved financial position in recent months, and, his talk about a future association. Back in his hotel room that evening, awaiting Elke's 8 PM call from Florence, Mike pondered the possible importance of these two facts.

What was Behrens up to, he kept asking himself. How had he come into his recent money? And what was he planning?

Mike decided to take a closer look at Behrens' personal activities. And he determined to start by checking Behrens' hotel room the next day. Perhaps something in the room, some papers possibly, would give him the answers. Yes, the next day, he'd have to search Behrens' room at the Excelsior.

He imagined it could be managed. Behrens, after all, probably wouldn't be staying in his room all day. He'd just have to be careful and make sure Behrens had gone out, before he tried his entry.

Mike looked at his watch. It was 8:15. Elke had said she would call at 8:00. But even as Mike was asking himself why Elke had not yet called, the telephone rang. Mike picked up the receiver.

"Hello," he said in English.

"Hello, Mike," Elke answered back.

"Elke. I was starting to get worried. You said you'd call at 8:00."

"Ah, it is so wonderful to have someone worry after me," Elke chided him.

Mike grumbled. "You know I wasn't too happy about letting you go up there alone. It's too damn dangerous."

"Oh, Mike," Elke said, "it is not dangerous in any way. I have merely gone and asked some questions today. And tomorrow, I will go to Milan and ask more questions. And then I will return to you. Nothing more. It is not dangerous at all."

"I'll feel better when you're back here. Now, tell me. What did you find out in Florence? Did Behrens stay at the Aprile?"

"Yes," Elke answered, her tone now serious. "I spoke with the concierge at great length. Behrens seems to stay at the Aprile whenever he is in Florence. And he was last here between August 20 and 26. The concierge looked it up for me in the register."

"Between August 20 and August 26," Mike repeated. "Yes. That fits with what the concierge at the Albergo Dante told me. And with the August 24th postmark on the Florence letter to Jacob Kaufman. Now, how about the typewriter?"

"That also fits," Elke answered. "First, I asked the concierge if Behrens ever rented a typewriter from him. And when he said Behrens did so, I asked to see it."

"And?"

"And it is the same typewriter that typed the Florence letter to Kaufman."

"You're sure?"

"I am certain. I will bring you back samples of what I typed today on that machine."

"Good. Very good," Mike said, pleased with the results of Elke's investigation. But he was still worried about Elke, herself. And he asked, "And nothing...nothing seemed unusual to you? You didn't have any trouble?"

"Nothing, Mike. Please. Stop worrying."

"That's hard to do."

"Oh, Mike. You are such a darling," Elke answered softly. Then, she spoke in a more businesslike tone. "I will leave for Milan tomorrow morning. I should have everything completed at the Albergo Tonale, there, by early afternoon."

"All right. Why don't you plan on calling me about 3:00 pm tomorrow, to let me know what you've found out," Mike suggested.

"That should be fine. It should give me enough time," Elke agreed. "And now, I am anxious to hear what you have been doing today. Did you get names of art dealers from Signor Veranti? And did you question them about Behrens?"

"Yes. I talked to 6 art dealers, to be exact. And I learned some interesting things," Mike answered reflectively.

"What? That is, if you can tell me?" Elke asked tentatively.

"Of course I can tell you," Mike shot back. "Hell, Elke. As far as I'm concerned, you're in this with me, all the way. Craig might not appreciate that. But there are a lot of things he doesn't have to know at this point!"

Elke giggled. "Including, even, the fact that you are working on the investigation at all?"

Mike grinned. "True enough." Then he turned serious. "But if it has to be that way for the time being, then those are the rules under which we operate. I can't stop before I nail Behrens and Zeitling!"

Then, he paused and subdued his feelings. And when he again spoke, it was in an unemotional tone.

"The main thing I found out today was actually something I had learned when I first started this investigation. Only it didn't register then."

"What is that?"

"It seems, all of the art dealers agree, that Behrens has come into some money in recent months. Probably a considerable amount. He's been dressing better. And as you know, he's moved into the Excelsior. You can't go much fancier than that."

"Yes? Has he had any particularly good art dealings, then?"

"No. And that's what is most interesting. All of the art dealers I spoke to today, they've all had dealings with Behrens over the last 10 or so years. But it's always been small stuff. He's not much of a factor in the art business here. Well, in the past several months, not only haven't these art dealers had *big* dealings with Behrens -- the kind that would account for his new wealth – they haven't done any business with him at all!

"And something else, too. Equally interesting and maybe more important. Behrens has also been doing some talking about the fact that he has a big business deal upcoming. That he'll be getting involved in the near future with some major gallery."

"Which one? Where?"

"No one knows."

There was a pause. "Well, Mike," Elke asked finally, "what do you think it all means?"

"I'm not sure, Elke. But I've got a strong feeling that whatever it means, I've got to find out. I think it's got to all be part of the picture."

"How are you going to find out? What will you do next?"

"I want to get into Behrens' room at the Excelsior. Maybe there's something there that'll give me some leads about this thing. About how he's been getting his money. Maybe in his personal papers…"

"Oh, Mike! Be careful. That is dangerous!"

"Not really," Mike assured Elke.

"But if he discovers you…"

"I'll make sure he's gone out. Now, don't worry any more about it. Please. Hell, Elke, you're the one I'm worried about. I still don't like your being up there alone."

"All right, Mike. A truce? I will stop mentioning that I am worried about you, and you will stop mentioning that you are worried about me. Until tomorrow night, when I will be back in Rome, and then we can worry together. It is agreed?"

In spite of his concern, Mike laughed. "Elke, I can hardly wait to stop worrying, together with you, tomorrow night."

"...I love you, Mike," Elke said.

"And I love you, Elke," Mike said.

There was a pause, and then Mike said, "Elke, did we just say something to each other that we never said before?"

"Yes, we did," Elke answered softly.

Another pause, and then Mike said, "we're going to have to talk more about this tomorrow night."

"I look forward to that," Elke said. "In the meantime, I will call you from Milan at 3:00 tomorrow afternoon."

CHAPTER TWENTY-FIVE

Elke had made train reservations for 8:30 in the morning. The run from Florence to Milan took a little over two hours, and she figured this would give her plenty of time to reach Milan, check what she had to at the Albergo Tonale, and call Mike by the agreed time of 3:00.

Now, the morning after she had spoken with Mike, Elke closed her small overnight bag and looked at her watch. It was 7:45 AM. Just right. Time enough to check out of the hotel, take a taxi to the station, and then, possibly have breakfast. Or, she could eat on the train.

Elke looked about the room, to make certain she had left nothing behind. Then she picked up the overnight bag and started for the door. No need to call room service. She had purposely taken only a small bag, so she could handle everything herself. It was a bit hard on the dress she was wearing for the second consecutive day. But the outfit traveled well, and it still looked quite fresh this morning. And besides, by tonight, she would be back in Rome.

Again, as she reached the door and started to open it, Elke turned and took a last look around the room. Thus it was, that with her back to the door, and being occupied in looking about the room, Elke did not see the two men who suddenly appeared in the doorway, blocking her exit.

CHAPTER TWENTY-SIX

At 9:30 the same morning, Mike had called the Excelsior, inquired as to the number of Signor Behrens' room, and had asked to be connected with him. He had held the receiver for a long interval, while the operator buzzed the room. But there had been no answer. Mike waited until the operator had returned to the line to ask if he wished to leave a message for Signor Behrens, who seemed to be out. Mike had replied in the negative and hung up.

Now, a short while later, he stood on the Via Veneto, on a corner opposite the Excelsior. Off to his right, and a bit farther down the Via Veneto, Mike could see the imposing U.S. Embassy building. He smiled wryly as he wondered what sort of a fit the ambassador and his staff might have right now, if they were to find out about Mike's unauthorized activities in relation to Jacob Kaufman and Otto Behrens. There'd be hell to pay. That was for sure.

Taking a deep breath to ease the tightness he was feeling in his stomach, Mike watched for a break in the traffic on the Via Veneto, and then dashed across the street. He walked up the broad sidewalk that led to the entrance of the Excelsior and went into the ornate lobby.

Signor Behrens, the telephone operator had informed him, was in room 743. Mike went to the bank of house phones and asked to be connected with 743. He waited while the telephone rang and went unanswered. Then, satisfied that Behrens wasn't in the room, he walked to the row of elevators and stepped into one of them.

As the elevator was guided upward by its operator, Mike reviewed what he hoped would be the successful way in which he would gain entry to Behrens' room. At the optimum, he hoped the room might be temporarily open, with one of the floor maids in attendance and cleaning up. A proper amount of money-passing, a conspiratorial wink and some mumblings about wanting to surprise Signor Behrens at a meeting they were to have shortly in the room, and Mike would probably be left alone for a while.

At the other, minimum end, the least promising alternative would be that he would have to break into the room by picking the lock. Mike felt confident he could do so, if necessary. As part of his wartime training in Army intelligence, he had learned how to pick locks. And in later years, he had kept up his facility as a sort of parlor game trick at parties. Also, the old fashioned locks of European hotels, so large and roomy, offered little resistance to even the most inept of lock pickers.

When the operator opened the elevator door, Mike stepped out onto the 7th floor and set off resolutely down the hallway toward the right. He continued walking until he heard the elevator door slide shut behind him. Then, he stopped and looked at the numbers on the nearest two consecutive doors. They told him that he was heading in the wrong direction, so he turned and began walking down the opposite hall.

Room 743 was located a considerable distance from the elevators and on another corridor. The hallway was deserted, and for that, Mike was thankful. At least if he had to pick the lock, the less traffic there was, the better.

He finally reached room 743. He stopped in front of the door and checked both ends of the corridor. No one in sight. He placed his hand on the doorknob and tried to turn it. It was locked. He'd have to break in.

Mike reached into his pocket and took out a small piece of celluloid he had purchased in anticipation of having to force the lock. Again checking both sides of the corridor to make sure no one was about, he bent toward the door and inserted the thin celluloid strip between the door and the door frame.

Slowly, he began probing for the lock mechanism. He experienced a couple of false starts, and he felt the perspiration begin to moisten his palms and forehead. Under his breath, he cursed his lack of practice. It had been a considerable time since he had entertained at any party by demonstrating his lock picking talents. And he realized now, too, that he had been stupid. He should have practiced the night before on the door of his own hotel room. At least, it would have given him a better feeling for what he was doing.

In the distance, Mike heard the sliding of the elevator door. A short pause, and he heard the door again. This time, he assumed it was closing. The question now, he thought, is whether somebody got off at this floor. And If so, was he heading in this direction?

At last! The celluloid strip was up against the lock mechanism. Mike cautiously started to apply pressure to the lock. Slowly, he manipulated the strip, careful not to abuse to delicate touch that was so necessary.

Suddenly, he became aware that someone had turned the corner at the far end of the corridor, and was walking toward him. Abruptly, Mike straightened up and gave the celluloid strip a final flick. The lock sprang, and Mike opened the door, at the same time hiding the celluloid piece in his hand. The other person was now almost abreast of him. Mike gave him a slight nod. The man returned it, and continued down the corridor. Mike stepped into the room and quickly closed the door.

Then, he leaned heavily against the wall and breathed deeply. He shook his head. That had been close. Too close. Fortunately, the corridor was a long one, so that the man hadn't seen the celluloid strip inserted into the lock, but probably assumed that Mike was using a key to get into his own room.

Mike now looked around the room. Quite a difference, he was sure, from what Behrens' accommodations must have been at the Albergo Dante. The room was richly appointed. The furniture was of excellent quality, although perhaps a bit too heavy in appearance for Mike's taste.

He pulled on a pair of gloves and walked over to a closed

door. He opened the door and saw several suits hanging on the rack. On the floor, there were four pairs of new looking shoes. And there were two suitcases on the overhead shelf.

He closed the closet door and walked to a bureau. It was bare on top. He opened the drawers and found various items of clothing, but nothing else.

Mike went to a second door in the room, opened it, and stepped into the bathroom. There was a cabinet over the washbowl, and he looked into it. It contained only a few bottles of what appeared to be common patent medicines.

Mike returned to the main room and looked around. It was comparatively bare. And so far, he had found nothing that would seem to be even the slightest bit useful to him. He looked again at the closet door, then walked to it and took out the larger of the two suitcases. Feeling its light weight, Mike guessed it was empty. He laid the suitcase on the bed and opened it. Yes, it was empty.

He returned the suitcase to the closet and reached for the second, smaller one. It was considerably heavier. Mike carried it over to the bed and put it down. He tried to open it, but it was locked.

"Damn," he hissed aloud.

If he wanted to see the contents, he'd have to pick the lock. And it would be a good deal tougher than the door lock.

He paused, weighing in his mind whether he should bother trying to open the suitcase. Was there anything important inside? Probably not. But on the other hand, why would Behrens lock it, unless it did contain something important? After all, nothing else in the room was under lock and key.

Mike decided to open the suitcase. He started to take a pen knife from his pocket when suddenly, there was a knock at the door, a key was inserted into the lock, and a woman's voice called in Italian, "Maid, Signore."

Mike grabbed the suitcase, ran to the closet and closed the door behind him, just before the maid came into the room. "Maid, Signore," she repeated, looking about.

Through a slight opening he had left in the closet door, Mike could see the maid. She seemed puzzled as she surveyed the made bed. "Hey, Rosa," she called out in Italian, turning her head toward the hallway. "Did you make this room already?"

"Number 743?" the unseen Rosa questioned from somewhere outside.

"Yeah. Number 743. It's all cleaned up."

"No. Not me," Rosa answered, now also entering the room and looking about. She walked over to the bathroom door and opened it. "Clean in here, too."

"How come?" the first maid asked. "This isn't a check out, is it?"

"No," Rosa assured her. "It's not on the list." She shrugged. "Paola must have cleaned it up."

The first maid snorted. "That stupid Paola. She's always getting things screwed up. Can't even remember what rooms she's supposed to clean. Goes and cleans one of mine, too."

"What're you complaining about?" Rosa asked. "It's one less room for you to do. So what's your complaint?"

The two maids left, closing the door behind them. Mike remained in the closet, listening to the sound of their chattering. Finally, their voices faded completely, and he came out of the closet.

He placed the suitcase on the bed and took out his pen knife. Luckily, the case had only a center lock, and no additional locks on the sides. Mike opened the thinnest and smallest blade on his knife, sat down on the edge of the bed, and began working on the lock.

It took him over 10 minutes to open the case. He could have done it a bit faster, but he didn't want to scratch the metal around the lock. He wanted to take every precaution to avoid having Behrens learn that his room had been searched.

When Mike finally got the suitcase open, he saw that its contents were a pile of papers. There seemed to be no particular order to the pile, and Mike began sifting through it.

For the most part, the papers were transactions of art sales, some correspondence with various art dealers, several old invoices and bills. Then, toward the bottom of the pile, Mike found a bank book from the Banco Nazionale del Romano. He opened it.

The first thing he noticed was that the book was comparatively new, with the initial entry having been made on July 21st, less than three full months before. That entry was a deposit for 1,875,000 lire. Mike did a fast and rough mental calculation. That was about 3,000 American dollars.

A second deposit had been made about three weeks later, on August 11th, that one for 1,560,000 lire. Again Mike calculated it. This was about $2,500 dollars.

Now, Mike checked the other deposit entries. There were only two of them. One, on September 10th, was for 2,500,000 lire. And the other, on October 5th, was for 1,875,000 lire. A total of about $12,500 American dollars for the four entries.

No wonder Behrens had started looking more prosperous to everyone. He *was* more prosperous. A hell of a lot so. And this $12,500 was only what he had in the bank, on deposit. He obviously had come into even more money than this, because he had been spending funds at a good clip. Rooms at the Excelsior, for example, did not come cheap.

Mike took out his pad, and jotted down the name of the bank, the account number, the dates of the deposits and the amounts. Quickly, he then looked through the remaining papers in the suitcase, but found nothing more of interest.

He put the papers back into the suitcase in the same order he had found them, shut the case, locked it and returned it to the closet shelf.

Then, he smoothed out the bedspread where the weight of the suitcase had wrinkled it slightly, and checked around the room to make sure nothing else was out of place. Everything was in order.

He walked to the door, listened to determine if it was quiet outside, and then he cautiously opened the door and looked out. The corridor was empty.

Mike stepped into it and closed the door, taking care to wipe the outside knob with his gloved hand. He pulled off the gloves, quickly folded them and put them into his coat pocket. Then he walked down the corridor toward the elevator.

CHAPTER TWENTY-SEVEN

Before Elke could scream or in any other way sound an alarm, the two men pushed her back into the hotel room. The smaller of the men held a knife at her throat, while with his other hand, he covered her mouth. The second man closed the door.

"You will be quiet," the small man warned, speaking in German and pushing the point of his knife against Elke's throat. "You will not scream when I take my hand away from your mouth. You understand?"

Fighting to control her terror, Elke nodded.

"Remember," the man warned, continuing to speak in German, "one scream, and it is over."

Again, Elke nodded, and the man removed his hand from her mouth.

She recognized the men as being Otto Behrens and Hans Zeitling, but she decided to attempt to bluff ignorance.

"What is it you want?" she said.

"If it is money, it is here, in my pocketbook..."

The sharp slap that Behrens delivered to her face threw Elke off balance and almost knocked her to the floor.

"Do not play games with us!" Behrens said roughly. "You know who we are and you know what we want." He leaned forward and raised his hand to strike her again. "The diary. Where is it? Where are you hiding it?"

"I...I do not have any diary," Elke answered, involuntarily flinching as Behrens' hand started toward her.

But instead of hitting her again, Behrens turned to Zeitling. "Look in her suitcase," he ordered. "Perhaps it is in there."

Zeitling picked up Elke's overnight bag, opened it, and dumped the contents on the bed. He began looking though the small pile.

"Anything?" Behrens asked.

"Nothing here," Zeitling answered, reaching next for Elke's large handbag and also dumping its contents on the bed. He looked through the assorted items. "And nothing here, either."

"So? Where is it?" Behrens demanded of Elke, as Zeitling again brought his knife against her throat. "Where is the diary?"

"Not anywhere that you can get it," Elke said defiantly, despite her fear.

Behrens studied her for a moment. Then he shrugged. "It is just as we assumed," he said to Zeitling. "I didn't think the diary would be with her. The American, Taylor, must have it. We will have to get it back from him."

Behrens roughly grasped Elke's chin in his hand. He smiled coldly as he looked at her. "And with such a tasty dish to offer in exchange, that should not be too difficult a task."

CHAPTER TWENTY-EIGHT

Mike looked again at the two columns of dates he had written on the piece of paper. The left hand column represented the dates of the postmarks of the four letters Jacob Kaufman had received from Milan, Paris, Florence and Rome. The right hand column had the dates of the deposits Otto Behrens had made.

It was obvious that the two columns were related. Within a week or two after each letter was sent to Kaufman, Behrens had made a sizeable deposit to his bank account.

The conclusion was a clear one. Clear, and yet, very puzzling. Jacob Kaufman, Mike theorized, must be paying blackmail to Otto Behrens.

The theory wasn't new to Mike at this point. He had been mulling it over for a few hours now, ever since returning to his hotel room after having searched Behrens' room.

In his own room, he had taken out the letters to Kaufman, and had copied down the dates of the postmarks in a column. Then, in an adjoining column, he had copied down the deposit dates. The parallels between the two columns had been obvious. And now, once again, Mike examined the validity of the conclusions he had drawn.

First, it seemed pretty definite that Kaufman was paying blackmail to Behrens. It would be even more conclusive, Mike knew, if he could somehow get a look at Kaufman's checking account and the withdrawals made from it. But that would be next to impossible. However, the pattern of the postmarks of the letters, and the dates of the deposits, strongly suggested the conclusion that blackmail was involved.

The second part of his theory, though, Mike knew, was the stickier one. And it had to do with the question of why Kaufman was paying blackmail money to Behrens?

When he had first asked himself this question a few hours ago, Mike hadn't found any answer. And then he remembered his last conversation with Craig.

At one point, Craig had told Mike that the reason Kaufman wanted to stop the investigation was that his daughter had somehow learned about it, and was very upset. And Mike remembered, too, what Kaufman had told him about his daughter, at their meeting in New York. Referring to the letters he had received, and to Mike's impending investigation, Kaufman had warned that "My daughter must never know of this, Mr. Taylor. I would rather die a thousand times by burning, than have my daughter learn of this. The consequences to her would be too dreadful to even contemplate!"

So dreadful, Mike now theorized grimly to himself, that

Kaufman was willing to pay blackmail indefinitely? So dreadful that, because his daughter had learned of this investigation, Kaufman had used whatever pressure he could, to stop it completely, even though he must have known that Behrens would then be in a position to financially bleed him to death!

The anger boiled in Mike as he thought about the vise within which Kaufman was being squeezed. A vise that was being pulled tighter and tighter by Behrens and Zeitling. He had to get them! He had to!

Mike turned from the window and began pacing about the room. There was something else he had to think about now, too. What to do about Craig?

Should he call Craig, and let him know what he had discovered in Behrens' room? Then, perhaps Craig would be able to present this new evidence to his superiors, and force a reopening of the investigation. If the investigation could be resumed on an official basis, then Mike knew that it would be a lot easier to get Behrens and Zeitling.

He rejected the idea. No. He couldn't take the chance. As far as Craig knew, he wasn't even working on the investigation. He was on vacation. And Mike sensed that if he brought Craig back into it now, there'd not only be hell to pay, but the investigation still wouldn't be started up again. And even more important, he'd be ordered back to the States on the first available plane, and that would be the end of the entire matter.

He'd have to keep going on his own, he concluded. He'd have

to bring together all the evidence he could, develop the strongest possible case, before letting Craig know what he was doing.

It seemed to Mike that one of the keys still was the need to link up Behrens and Zeitling with the diary. To establish beyond any doubt that they were Captain Max Schmidt and Corporal Hans Zeitling of Dachau. Then, they could be nailed as Nazi war criminals. And Kaufman, and his fear and concern for his daughter, could even be kept out of it entirely. Behrens and Zeitling would be tried strictly as war criminals. The blackmail matter wouldn't even have to be mentioned.

Thinking about the evidence he had to build against Behrens and Zeitling, Mike's mind turned next to Elke, as he wondered what she had discovered in Milan. He looked at his watch and was surprised to see that it was already 3:30. Elke was supposed to have called at about 3:00. Well, she'd probably be calling shortly.

CHAPTER TWENTY-NINE

Elke strained at the ropes that tied her hands and feet to the bed frame. But she couldn't loosen the bindings. She wondered what time it was. She could tell by the deepening shadows that it was early evening, but she had no idea of the exact time.

So much had happened since the morning, perhaps only 12 hours or so ago, when Behrens and Zeitling had accosted her at the hotel.

Following their questioning of her, they had accompanied Elke as she checked out, and then they had started back to Rome in a car, Zeitling driving, and she wedged between the two men.

Behrens had warned Elke not to try and make contact with anyone along the way. And to reinforce the warning, he had kept Zeitling's knife against her stomach, though out of sight of other motorists or pedestrians.

As they neared Rome, Zeitling had pulled the car off the Autostrada and stopped. "All right," Behrens ordered Elke, "into the back of the car."

Elke got into the back seat and Behrens followed her.

"Turn around," he told her. When she did, Behrens pulled Elke's hands behind her back and tied them. Next, he placed a gag in her mouth, and then he blindfolded her. "Now," he said, shoving her, "get down on the floor."

After that, Elke had no way of knowing where they went, although she guessed that they had entered Rome because of the increased traffic noise. And she suspected, too, that their destination was one of the hills that dotted the outskirts of the city. She drew this conclusion because of the climb the car made shortly before it came to a stop.

"Anyone on the street?" Elke heard Behrens ask.

"No one," Zeitling answered.

"Out," Behrens ordered, pulling Elke from the car.

Once on the street, Zeitling and Behrens got on either side of Elke and half carried, half dragged her across what seemed a very narrow sidewalk and then into a building. They went down a short hall and entered the elevator. After what seemed to Elke a short ride upward, they got out of the elevator, went down another hall, and entered an apartment.

Still blindfolded, Elke was guided through another door and then pushed down onto the bed, where her hands and feet were tied to the frame. Only then was the blindfold removed, and Elke found herself in the bedroom she now occupied. They had left the gag in her mouth.

Since being tied to the bed, Elke had neither seen nor heard Zeitling and Behrens. The two men had gone into the next room, and their conversation had been muffled by the closed door. After a while, Elke had heard a door open and close, followed by silence. And whether one or both of them had gone out, she could not tell.

In the ensuing time, Elke had repeatedly tried to untie the ropes, but had made no headway at all. She had also thought about Mike, and what he might be doing. He had expected her to call at 3:00, she knew. Was he alarmed by now because she hadn't called? Was he at all suspicious yet?

The involuntary tears pushed out of Elke's eyes and trickled down her cheeks. Even if Mike's suspicions were aroused, what good would it do? How could he ever find her? She was frightened. So frightened!

CHAPTER THIRTY

Mike waited for Elke's call until 5:00, telling himself that he was silly to imagine that anything was wrong. But when she hadn't called by 5:00, he decided to try and reach her.

He placed a call to the concierge at the Albergo Tonale in Milan, the hotel where Behrens was supposed to have stayed.

No, the concierge told him. No young lady, German or otherwise, had been in to see him at any time that day, to inquire about a Signore Behrens. Yes, he had been on duty ever since 10:00 in the morning. No, he was absolutely sure. Absolutely.

Next, Mike placed a call to the hotel in Florence where Elke had stayed the night before.

Yes, he was told by the concierge, Miss Herrman had checked out early that morning, about 8:00, in fact. No, She had not been heard from since, and she had not left any messages for him.

"Had anything seemed wrong or unusual with Miss Herrman," Mike asked the concierge, explaining that Miss Herrman was supposed to have called him, but had not, and he was worried about her.

"No, there hadn't seemed to be anything wrong. She and her companions had seemed perfectly normal."

"Companions!" Mike interrupted the concierge. "Who were the companions?"

"There were two men with her," the concierge explained to Mike. "Two men with Miss Herrman at the time she checked out."

Reluctantly, and already sensing what the answer would be, Mike asked the concierge to describe the two men. As he listened, his fears were confirmed. It was Behrens and Zeitling! No doubt about it.

Mike hung up, and then quickly picked up the telephone again and placed a call to the Hotel Excelsior. He asked to be connected with Otto Behrens' room.

After a short pause, the operator came back on the line. "I am sorry," she told him, "But Signore Behrens is no longer in the hotel."

"When did he check out? What time?"

"At 4:00," the operator answered. "Just over one hour ago."

"Did he leave any forwarding address?"

"No. No forwarding address."

Mike felt the tightness grip at his stomach. First, Behrens and Zeitling had been with Elke in Milan. And next, Behrens had checked out of the Excelsior. What did it mean? And what danger was Elke in?

CHAPTER THIRTY-ONE

Elke heard a door open and then close, followed by footsteps coming in her direction. She looked toward the door of the bedroom as it opened. It was Zeitling.

"Still safe and secure?" he asked with cold humor. "Is our little pigeon still safe and secure in her nest?" He came over to the bed and took out her gag. Elke stiffened as Zeitling placed his hand on her breast and caressed it. "Under other circumstances, Little Pigeon," he said, his eyes showing his hunger, "you would be a tempting morsel. Right here, on this bed."

"Pig!" Elke spat out the word. "You were a pig at Dachau, and you are still a pig today!"

Zeitling drew his hand away and looked sharply at Elke. Then he smiled. "You are quite the reader, aren't you? Quite a reader of diaries."

"I don't have to read a diary to know your kind," Elke answered. "The kind that has made me ashamed at times of being German."

"Quiet, Little Pigeon," Zeitling warned. "Quiet, before I cut up that pretty face of yours." Then he smiled again.

"Yes, you and your American are quite the readers of diaries." The smile disappeared. "But it would have been far better for both of you, if you had never read that diary. If you had never laid eyes on it." He shrugged. "However, it does not make any difference, now."

"What do you mean?"

"I mean, we will soon have the diary back. Your American will shortly be returning that diary to us."

"You will never get it back!"

Zeitling smiled and bent close to Elke, as he put the gag back in her mouth. "I think we will, Little Pigeon, I think we will."

CHAPTER THIRTY-TWO

Mike considered his alternatives. He could go to the Rome police and ask them for help in finding Elke. But that wasn't a good idea. For one thing, he wasn't even sure Elke was in Rome. Behrens and Zeitling might have her hidden somewhere else.

And what would he tell the Rome police? All he had to go on were a bunch of conjectures and half-finished theories. And being a foreigner, how seriously would he be taken?

And finally, if, by showing his government credentials he was able to convince the police that what he was saying was worth investigation, they'd certainly first check with the U.S. Embassy. Then it would very quickly get back to Craig.

So, what next? What to do next?

He had to find Behrens. That was the only thing that made sense. Behrens was back in Rome. That was definite, since he had checked out of the Excelsior only an hour ago. Find Behrens and he'd be able to find out where Elke was.

But where could Behrens be? And was Zeitling with him? And did they have Elke in the same place?

Or was she being kept somewhere else?

Mike probed his mind for possible leads, clues, impulses, anything that seemed even remotely realistic a starting point. Finally, he turned and hurried for the door. It was a real long shot, but worth trying.

....

A short while later, Mike entered the lobby of the Albergo Dante. He had gone to the Dante, not because he thought Behrens might have checked back into the place after leaving the Excelsior. But because he wanted to question the concierge again, and perhaps somehow turn up some clues as to Behrens' habits. Where did he usually eat? Where did he go in the evening?

Mike hoped the concierge would be able to give him some information. Enough, at least, to enable him to go on to another source, where he could ask more questions about Behrens. And eventually, hopefully, he would have enough of a pattern to Behrens' activities to be able to find him. It was a thin hope, Mike knew. But it was all he had to go on at the moment.

He looked anxiously toward the concierge's station. Luck was with him. On duty was the same concierge he had questioned the first time he had come to the Dante.

The concierge recognized him. "Signore," he greeted Mike. "It is good to see you again. You are still searching for information about Signor Behrens and his lady friend?" he asked slyly.

Mike smiled at the concierge. "Yes. Still searching for more information. You haven't seen Signore Behrens recently, have you?"

The concierge shook his head. "No. Not since he checked out, which was even before you came to question me that first time. No. I have not seen him since."

"Has he possibly called here today? Or has anyone come to inquire about him?" Mike asked.

"No. No one. But you know, I am glad that you have come back, because there is something else I have to tell you."

"What's that?"

"After you and I spoke last time, another person came here. The little man. The one I told you had visited Signor Behrens?"

"He came after I was here?"

"Si."

Mike took out the picture of Hans Zeitling. "Is this the man? It's an old picture, but he still looks very much like this today. Is this the man who visited Signor Behrens, and who then came here, after me?"

The concierge looked at the picture. "Si. He is the one. And he had many questions to ask about you."

"About me?"

"Si. He wanted to know all about what you and I had spoken. Of course, I told him nothing. You understand that." The concierge made a distasteful face. "I would never tell a German anything."

The revelation that Zeitling had followed him to the Albergo Dante didn't surprise Mike. By now, he was certain that Behrens and Zeitling somehow had been on to him almost from the time he had arrived in Rome. He decided to start asking the concierge the questions he had come here for.

"Tell me this, Signore," Mike began, "while Signor Behrens was living here, did he seem to have any favorite restaurants where he often went to eat?"

The concierge thought for a moment. "I do not know. I never saw him in any of the places right around this section."

"What about favorite night clubs? Or cafés? Any place where he might have spent his evenings?"

The concierge threw up his hands in a gesture of frustration. "I simply do not know. Signor Behrens, as much as I am able to tell, did not have any such favorite places."

"Well," Mike asked in desperation, "Was there anything that he seemed to do on a regular basis? Any habit of his which would mean his going to the same place almost every night?"

The concierge shook his head. "No, Signore. There was nothing that I could see."

Mike asked, "The last time the man came here? The one who was asking questions about me? Did he leave you any address or telephone number where you could find him, if you wanted to give him information?"

"No. He left nothing. No address. No telephone number."

For the time being, Mike was stumped. He took out his note pad and wrote down the name of his hotel on a piece of paper. "If that man comes back here again," he told the concierge, handing him the piece of paper, "or, if you remember anything else, I would appreciate you calling me."

"Si, Signore," the concierge answered, taking the slip of paper. "And I am only sorry that I could not be of more help now. I am sorry, Signore."

CHAPTER THIRTY-THREE

As the door to the bedroom opened, Elke stiffened, expecting it to be Zeitling again. This time, though, it was Behrens.

He came in and briefly looked at her, expressionless. Then he left the room. He didn't close the door behind him, however, and Elke was able to hear the ensuing conversation.

"She give you any trouble while I was away?" Behrens asked.

"No," Zeitling assured him. "Are you all checked out now?"

"Yes. No trace left, so we can go ahead with the next step. Do you have the note written?"

"It's all done," Zeitling replied. "It should bring him running."

"Let me see it," Behrens said. He took the note from Zeitling and read it aloud. "If you wish to see Elke Herrman alive, you will bring the diary to the bridge that connects with the Isola Tiberina. You will walk across the bridge to the center, at the island, where you will be contacted. You will start your walk across the bridge at 1:30 AM. No tricks. Come alone. You will be observed. Do not inform the police in any way. No tricks, or you will never see Elke Herrman alive again.

This is the only message you will receive, so you better be at the bridge on time. Remember, no police, or Elke Herrman dies."

Behrens looked up from the note and addressed Zeitling. "Yes, that ought to bring him running. Americans are very sentimental. Anything to save a woman's life." He thought for a moment, then spoke again. "You're sure you can surprise him?" he asked Zeitling. "And you're sure no one will see you?"

"Yes, I am sure," Zeitling assured Behrens. "There is never a soul around there at that hour. And as for surprising him," he smiled, "He will never make it to the center of the island. He has to pass near some dark doorways first. And that's where I will get him."

"You are certain?" Behrens persisted.

"That bridge is so narrow that even if he walks right in the center of the road, he still is not very far from the doorways of the buildings. One good leap, and I've got him. Right in the heart."

"All right. And then as soon as you've got the diary…"

"As soon as I've got the diary," Zeitling picked up the thought, "I'll be back here. Then, I'll take care of our friend in the bedroom."

Behrens nodded. "You better deliver the note now," he said.

Zeitling reached for his hat and coat. "I will be back soon." He nodded toward the bedroom. "Perhaps you might check on her every once in a while? Make sure she doesn't loosen her ropes?"

"Yes," Behrens agreed.

He watched Zeitling leave the apartment. Then he turned and

went into the bedroom. He looked at Elke.

"You're not trying anything foolish, are you?" he asked quietly.

He walked over to the bed and checked the ropes that held Elke's hands and feet to the frame. Satisfied the bindings were secure Behrens turned and left.

Elke twisted her hands helplessly. They were held fast. She could feel the skin growing raw where she had been trying to break loose. No. It was no use!

But she had to find a way! She had to find a way to warn Mike. To tell him to keep away from Isola Tiberina. Zeitling was going to kill him!

CHAPTER THIRTY-FOUR

By the time Mike returned to his hotel, it was after 9:30 in the evening. He returned reluctantly. But for the moment, he had to return. It was simple enough. He didn't know where else to go. Where else to look for Elke. Or more specifically, Behrens.

After leaving the Albergo Dante, Mike had called on the ever helpful Dr. Veranti of the Rome Art Dealers Association. But this time, Dr. Veranti couldn't assist him. No, he had no idea where Behrens might have gone, now that he had checked out of the Excelsior. And, as far as he knew, there were no gallery openings or receptions scheduled for that evening, or for the next two evenings, in fact.

Mike next went to see each of the art dealers he had questioned the day before about Behrens. But none of them could give him any leads as to where he might now find Behrens.

And then finally, in desperation, Mike had wandered about the Via di Babuino for a time, peering into the various galleries and art shops, in the wild hope that he might see Behrens in one of them. But nothing.

Finally, then, Mike had decided to return to the hotel. Now, as he entered the lobby and approached the desk for his key, the concierge called out to him.

"Signor Taylor."

"Yes?" Mike responded dully.

"Signor Taylor. This came for you a few hours ago, with instructions to give it to you as soon as possible."

Mike quickly grabbed the envelope the concierge offered him. He ripped it open and unfolded the paper that was inside.

As he read the note, Mike's face turned grim and his hands tightly clenched the paper.

"Is something wrong, Signore Taylor?" the concierge asked with concern.

"No. Nothing's wrong," Mike quickly assured him. He decided he'd better get to his room, where he could think things out in privacy. He walked quickly toward the elevator.

A few moments later, in his room, Mike made his decision after having read the note several times. He'd have to comply with its terms. There was little else he could do. Too much was at stake, otherwise. Specifically, Elke's life.

For an instant, he thought about going to the meeting place, but leaving the diary in the hotel safe, where it was now. But no. That was too much of a risk of Elke's life. The only important thing was to save her. And the note was clear enough in its threat on that point: "No tricks, or you will never see Elke Herrman alive again." No, As much as he wanted the diary, because it was his best evidence against Behrens and Zeitling, he wanted Elke's safety more. So, he'd bring the diary with him.

Mike looked at his watch. It was 9:50. He wouldn't have to leave the hotel until at least 12:45. Impatiently, he began pacing about the room.

CHAPTER THIRTY-FIVE

The Rome night air coming off the Tiber River had a nip to it that made Mike hunch his shoulders slightly as he stood on the Lungarno di Pierleoni. He had just dismissed the taxi that had brought him from his hotel. And now, he turned and looked down the tree lined thoroughfare. The street, so thick with traffic during the day, was almost empty. Only an occasional car sped past him.

Ahead, Mike could see the silhouette of the Isola Tiberina bridge, the narrow crossing over the Tiber River that connected the Trastevere section of Rome with the rest of the city. He looked at his watch. It was 1:25 AM. He put his hand in his coat pocket and felt the diary. This was the ransom that the note had demanded in exchange for Elke's life.

Mike's lips set tightly against each other as he thought of this ransom, and of the hope it held for Elke's safe return. Whoever had written the note, and Mike was sure it was Behrens and Zeitling, although it had been unsigned, had promised Elke wouldn't be hurt. They had better keep that promise, Mike vowed to himself, or they'd be eternally sorry.

He wondered which of the two men, Behrens or Zeitling, would be meeting him at the center of the bridge. Perhaps both of them? Or, even possibly an emissary of theirs? He took a deep breath. Well, he'd find out soon enough. He started walking down the Lungarno di Pierleoni toward the bridge.

CHAPTER THIRTY-SIX

Behrens looked at his watch and then walked from the living room into the bedroom. He came over to the bed, and while checking the ropes that bound Elke, he addressed her.

"Our time together will soon be ending, Miss Herrman." He sighed. "Ah, but that our meeting might have been under different circumstances. After all, a beautiful young German girl like you…"

Elke, gagged, stared wordlessly back at Behrens. He reached down and took the gag out. Elke ran her tongue over the dry and cracked lining of her mouth. Then she looked up at Behrens, the hate apparent in her face.

"You make me ill," she told him. "You and your companion both make me ill!"

Behrens smiled. "I admit Zeitling leaves much to be desired," he answered her with amusement. "But such are the demands of business, that one cannot always choose their associations, no matter how much they offend the sensibilities."

"What do you know of sensibilities," Elke said. "Where were your sensibilities during the war? Amidst all of the slaughter?

Where were your sensibilities then?"

"I don't know what you're talking about," Behrens snapped back. "What I did during the war was my duty only." Then he smiled again. "And it was harmless enough at that. Mostly dull, too. All those records." He shook his head. "Sometimes I think that if the German people ever cease to exist, the only epitaph they will leave behind is a mountain of records."

The callousness of Behrens' words disgusted Elke. She wondered how he could be so cold as to refer to the slaughter at Dachau as, harmless and dull. Aloud, she taunted him. "Records like the diary?"

"Like the diary," Behrens echoed. He shook his head. "A most unfortunate record that should have been destroyed." He shrugged. "But no matter." He looked at his watch. "Shortly, it will be destroyed. Once and for all, along with your Mr. Taylor."

"You will never succeed," Elke said. "Others will find you out. You will never succeed."

"Ah, but Miss Herrman," Behrens countered good-naturedly, "I already have succeeded. And for the future, nothing but even more success. Of that I am sure." He again looked at his watch. "As a matter of fact, thanks to Zeitling and his sure knife, the latest step in the successful epoch should now be just about ready to be taken. Namely, the death of Mr. Taylor."

CHAPTER THIRTY-SEVEN

It was 1:30, exactly, as Mike reached the foot of the Isola Tiberina bridge. The few street lamps implanted on the bridge glowed only feebly, so that most of the structure was in darkness.

They picked a damn good place for the meeting, Mike admitted grudgingly to himself. He paused for a moment and looked to both sides. The Lungarno di Pierleoni was deserted. Now, not even an occasional car passed. He looked in front of him, across the small stone bridge. There was no movement visible. All the lights were out in the apartments in the buildings on the bridge.

With his eyes, Mike measured the width of the street crossing the bridge. Perhaps 6 or 7 feet. Almost just a foot path. Next, he looked at the two rows of small buildings that bordered the bridge at its center, shrouding it in almost total darkness. That would be an ideal spot, he figured, for an assault, if that were Behrens' and Zeitling's plan. Of course, he couldn't be sure, but he'd have to be alert to the possibility. And besides, he had his own plans about the meeting. Even though he had brought the diary with him, he hoped to use it only as bait. He hoped to overpower whoever he was meeting, and force him to reveal where Elke was being kept.

Mike slipped his right hand into his suit jacket and closed his fingers around the handle of his gun. Then, slowly, he started up the bridge. He walked in the center of the street, although he realized that this made him a clear target. But he decided this was better than walking near the shadowed walls of the buildings, from which an assailant could more easily attack him.

From his hiding place in the doorway of one of the buildings, Zeitling watched Mike's approach. He had carefully selected this location. The doorway was part of an apartment building that jutted out into the street somewhat, making it one of the narrowest points on the bridge. It was no more than 6 feet from wall to wall, Zeitling estimated.

With an experienced ease, Zeitling held his knife loosely in his right hand, while he flexed the fingers on his left hand. He was standing on the left side of the bridge. His plan was to let the American walk just past him. Then, quickly, silently, he would leap from his hiding place. With his left arm, he would encircle the American's left shoulder. With his left hand, he would cover Taylor's mouth, minimizing the chances of a scream. And almost at the same instant, with his right hand, he would plunge the knife into the American's heart, taking care, to avoid the ribs.

It was the classic knife assault from behind, and Zeitling anticipated no trouble in accomplishing it. After all, hadn't he practiced it enough times on the Jews at Dachau?

He tightened his fingers on the knife handle, as he watched the American, walking slowly and cautiously, and drawing nearer.

Mike was almost at the center of the bridge, now. He stopped. Still no sign of the person he was supposed to meet. No sign of anything, in fact. Nothing moving. Nothing standing out from the almost total darkness. He turned his head slowly from side to side. Nothing.

A few feet away, withdrawn into the doorway, Zeitling watched. His body was tensed. He was balanced on his toes, ready to pounce as soon as the American had passed him. He held his eyes steadily on the left side of Mike's chest, fixing in his mind the spot where he would drive the knife.

Mike started moving again, slowly. He was almost abreast of Zeitling now, and the German raised his knife up and leaned forward on his toes, preparatory to leaping. Just another foot or two now...

The sudden wail of a baby's anguished cry broke the silence just as Zeitling began his move toward Mike's back. Mike whirled at the sound of the baby's cry and saw Zeitling. Zeitling tried to regain control of his body, tried to stop his forward momentum, realizing that he had lost his most valuable advantage, the element of surprise.

But he and Mike came together. Mike saw Zeitling's right arm coming toward him, knife in hand. Mike shot his left arm up, hoping to block the forward progress of Zeitling's arm.

The force of Zeitling's leap knocked Mike to the ground, with the other man coming down with him.

With the intense and continued crying of the baby providing a tempoed accompaniment, Mike and Zeitling struggled in the darkness. Mike felt a sudden and agonizing pain in his groin as Zeitling dug his knee in. In an instant, the German was atop him, bringing the knife downward. Again, Mike grasped Zeitling's wrist, slowing the progress of the knife.

For several seconds, they remained in this position, Zeitling straining to push the knife toward Mike's breast, Mike resisting with all his strength.

Then, slowly, but with certainty, their positions started to change. As in a melting wax tableau, the figures began to sway into a new arrangement. Mike was bending Zeitling to the side now, so that as the two bodies rolled, it was Mike who was emerging on top.

Zeitling tried again to drive his knee into Mike's groin. But this time, Mike was able to block him with a vicious twist. That maneuver completed the intensity of Zeitling's knife thrust. Now, however, with their positions reversed, it was Zeitling's breast that the knife penetrated, digging in deeply.

Zeitling started convulsing. Mike kept the knife in, twisting and turning it, until Zeitling stopped moving. Then he jumped up and dragged the body into the same doorway from which Zeitling had leaped, a moment before.

As the baby continued to cry from an apartment somewhere above him, Mike took out a small flashlight and trained it on his assailant's face. It was Zeitling, he confirmed and it was obvious that he was dead.

Damn! Mike cursed to himself. Now, how would he find Elke? He had hoped to overpower whoever he was meeting. And then force him to reveal where Elke was being kept. But he hadn't anticipated having to kill the person.

Mike bent over the body and searched Zeitling's pockets, looking for the man's wallet. He located it, and quickly dumped its contents on the ground. Then he found it! What he had hoped might be in the wallet. He read the slip of paper. It was a receipt for rent paid on a furnished apartment at Via Premuda, Number 7. And it was dated only one week ago!

Mike went through the rest of Zeitling's pockets, taking out everything, and putting the items into his own pockets. Later, he would dump it all in a garbage can, far removed from the scene. The main thing now, though, was that he did not want Zeitling to be immediately identified by the police. He didn't want Behrens to be alerted to Zeitling's death, to possibly read about it in the papers. At least not until Elke was safe.

Mike looked out on the bridge. It was empty. No one about. He stepped from the doorway and walked quickly back toward the Lungarno di Pierleoni. He wanted to get to Zeitling's apartment as quickly as possible, hoping that Elke would be there.

But he realized that he had better walk a few blocks before hailing a cab. At this time of night, the cab driver might remember him, if Zeitling's picture hit the papers, and might remember, too, where he had picked him up. Mike wanted to avoid the possibility of this happening.

CHAPTER THIRTY-EIGHT

Elke lay still on the bed, no longer struggling against the ropes that bound her. It must be over by now, she felt. Zeitling had left the apartment long ago. By now, he must have killed Mike. Mike was dead, and nothing else mattered.

She realized now that they had been foolish to try and do everything themselves. They should have brought the officials into it. Despite all of the political pressures involved, they should have alerted the officials. Then, Elke thought bitterly to herself, Mike would still be alive.

Elke knew, too, that she was going to die in a few minutes. As soon as Zeitling returned. But she didn't care. She was already dead. Drained by exhaustion, and by sorrow over Mike's murder.

Behrens came back into the room. He took the gag out of her mouth.

"In a few minutes, Zeitling will return, Miss Herrman," he said to her. "And then it will be your turn."

Elke didn't answer him.

Behrens smiled. "What?" he asked. "No response this time?

No more vows to make?"

"Leave me alone," Elke begged.

Behrens laughed. "Leave you alone. Leave you alone." He leaned toward Elke, his face hovering above hers. "You foolish person! If you and your American friend had only left me alone before, you would not be here now. You are a foolish person, to have mixed into something that was of no concern to you!"

Now, Behrens' calm demeanor was shattered. His face was livid. The veins at his temples throbbed as he looked down at Elke, and the hatred was clearly evident in his features.

Elke imagine that this was how the man must have looked to many of his victims at Dachau, just before he killed them. "Beast!" she shouted at him. "Beast!"

She spat in Behrens' face and he involuntarily drew back. Then he came forward again, his hand raised to strike her. Elke closed her eyes and turned her head to avert the blow.

But it never came. Instead, she heard Mike shout her name, and when she opened her eyes, she saw Mike and Behrens struggling.

"Mike!" she screamed in warning, as she saw Behrens raise the heavy ash tray that he had grabbed from the bureau. He swung it toward Mike's head. Alerted by Elke, Mike managed to avert the blow, but only partially, and as the ash tray grazed him, he fell stunned.

For a second, Behrens stood still, undecided, looking from the stunned and temporarily immobile Mike, to the bound Elke.

Elke began to scream as loudly as she could, and with this, Behrens made up his mind. Turning, he ran from the room and the apartment.

"Mike! Mike! Mike!" Elke sobbed at his motionless body. She strained against her ropes, but could not loosen them.

Then, Mike began to move. Eagerly, Elke watched as he opened his eyes and shook his head. "Mike," she called hopefully.

From his place on the floor, Mike turned his head toward the sound of Elke's voice. With difficulty, he finally managed to focus his eyes until he saw her clearly. Then, he put his hand to the spot on his head where the ash tray had hit him. He examined his hand. Weakly, he grinned up at Elke. "Well, no blood, so I guess I'm still alive," he said, "even though you do look like a bona fide, real heavenly angel to me right now."

"Oh, Mike," Elke cried. "Oh, Mike," she kept repeating, as he sat on the floor, recovering his senses.

"You are all right, aren't you, Mike?" Elke asked anxiously a few moments later, as Mike was untying her.

By now, Mike was fully recovered. "yes," he assured her. "I'm all right now." He took her hands in his. "But you, you poor kid, You've had a hell of a time, haven't you?"

"The worst was when I thought Zeitling had killed you," Elke answered. "It was so awful. Hearing them plan your death. Even knowing the time of it. And not being able to do anything."

"You sure tried like hell," Mike said, examining the raw skin on Elke's wrists where she had attempted to break loose of the ropes. "They must hurt terribly."

"Not with you holding them," she smiled up at him.

"That's my girl," he answered, kissing her.

"What do we do now, Mike?" Elke asked, "what do we do about Behrens? And Zeitling? What happened to him?"

"Zeitling's dead," Mike told her.

"You...you had to kill him?" Elke asked.

"Yes," Mike replied, as he helped Elke to her feet. He steadied her until she was able to stand alone. "As for Behrens, I don't really know how much more we can do about him on our own."

"You mean we should inform the Rome police now?"

Mike shook his head. "No. Not quite. Hell, then there'd be all sorts of complications." He smiled wryly at her. "Not the least of which is my killing Zeitling."

"But that was self-defense."

"Yes. Sure. But go explain it. And explain why I was meeting him on that bridge at 1:30 in the morning. And why I didn't notify the police as soon as I had killed him. And why I stripped him of all identification papers."

Elke nodded. "I see what you mean." She thought for a moment. "But then, what do we do? Do we look for Behrens ourselves? Here in Rome?"

Mike shook his head. "No. I don't think so. Hell. We'd never find him. For all we know, he's probably already on his way out of Rome, going somewhere else. No. Without official help, we couldn't possibly find him how." He thought for a moment. "So, what we're going to do, is go right back to the source on this. The place where it all started."

"The place where it all started?"

"Right. Back to the United States. And more specifically, Craig and then Jacob Kaufman. That's the only way to find Behrens. I've got to convince Craig that it's worth opening the investigation again, officially. And I've got to make Kaufman agree to that. It's the only way."

"Am…am I coming with you?" Elke asked hesitantly.

Mike looked at her. "You bet you are," he said tenderly. Then, he turned and began walking about the bedroom. "But first, let's give this place a going over. Maybe we can turn up something that'll be useful to us."

For the next several minutes, Mike and Elke methodically searched the apartment. They began in the bedroom, but found nothing of interest there.

The only other rooms in the apartment were the small kitchen, the even tinier bathroom, and the living room. Elke watched as Mike searched the first two of these room, but found nothing. Then, together, they searched the living room, working their way, finally, to the last piece of furniture in the room, a desk in one of the corners.

With Elke standing by, Mike opened the main drawer of the desk and looked in at the contents. They were sparse. Just a few papers. Mike picked up the pile and began going through it. He paused when he came to a torn piece of paper which seemed to be part of a typewritten sheet. The writing was in German.

"What is it, Mike?" Elke asked.

"It seems to be part of a letter, or a note," Mike answered, examining the contents. "And it's about us!"

"Us?"

"Yes," Mike replied. "I don't know what the rest of the pages says, but starting with the top line on this piece of paper, it's a continuation of a sentence. And here's where it picks up." Mike started to read aloud, translating from the German as he went. "… and so you must get the diary, and just as important, you must certainly kill them, the American and the German. The threat to our safety is too great. Use whatever means are necessary. It is most important."

Mike looked at Elke. "That's all there is."

"Nothing more?"

"Nothing more," Mike repeated, as he closely examined the piece of paper. It was a high grade quality of bond paper, slightly blue in color, like personalized stationery, and with part of a distinctively designed watermark visible near its jagged top.

Carefully, Mike folded the paper and put it in his pocket. Then he smiled at Elke. "Well, Zeitling certainly wasn't very good at following Behrens' orders, was he?" he said. "We've still got the diary, and we're both still alive, the American and the German."

Then, the smile left Mike's face. "And we'll get him," he vowed. "If we can just convince Craig – and Kaufman – to reopen the investigation, we'll get Behrens!"

CHAPTER THIRTY-NINE

"Taylor, you must be completely out of your mind!"

The speaker was William Craig. Listening were Mike and Elke. They were seated in Craig's office in New York only hours after having left Zeitling's apartment in Rome.

In those intervening hours, Elke and Mike had checked out of their Rome hotel and booked passage on a 10:00 AM Alitalia flight to New York. They had arrived 8 hours later, shortly after 12 noon, New York time. Clearing customs, they had taken a taxi from Kennedy International Airport, directly to Craig's office at 120 Broadway in Manhattan.

Craig had just returned from lunch. Mike started to tell him his story, but had gotten only so far as to say that he and Elke had been continuing the investigation, and that he felt it was imperative to approach Jacob Kaufman and urgently try to get the matter reopened. It was at that point that Craig had burst out with his comment, which he now repeated.

"Yes, you must be completely out of your mind," the intense anger evident in his voice.

"Taylor, you'd better have an awfully good explanation to give me, or you'll be in so much trouble, you'll never get out," he warned.

"You've disobeyed every order in the book. You continued the investigation when you weren't supposed to. You deliberately broke the confidential status of this case wide open by bringing Miss Herrman into it. And God only knows what else you've done!"

Craig reached across his desk and flipped one of the buttons on his intercom. "Don't disturb me until further notice," he ordered his secretary. Then, he glared at Mike. "Okay, let's have it," he snapped. "Right from the beginning, up until you got here."

Carefully, slowly, Mike gave Craig the details. From time to time, he checked his note pad. Occasionally, he looked to Elke for confirmation of a fact, but he never asked her to speak. And at a few points in the narrative, he offered Craig various pieces of evidence. These included the diary, which he and Elke had marked in several pertinent places, the piece of note paper they had found in Zeitling's apartment, the photo of Zeitling, and the record of bank deposits Mike had copied from Behrens' bank book.

Mike concluded his report by describing the previous night's events in Rome. He pointed out to Craig that he strongly felt the only way Behrens would now ever be tracked down, was with official government aid, both American and German. He also stressed that aside from any blackmail activities Behrens had been conducting against Jacob Kaufman, he also was a Nazi war criminal, and should be brought to trial on that count, if nothing else.

For a considerable time after Mike finished, the room was still. Craig, seemingly oblivious to their presence, turned his swivel chair and stared out the window. Elke looked at Mike and gave him an encouraging smile.

Finally, Craig spun to face them. "When you get right down to it, Taylor, the facts are pretty bad. You've gathered nothing but a bunch of suspicions and circumstantial evidence. And on that basis, you disregarded top secret security orders that involved not only your own government, but the German government as well. You discovered a murdered man in Paris, and didn't report that murder to the police. And you killed a man in Rome, stripped his body of identification, and did not report it to the police. In essence, you're now a fugitive from Rome!"

"But he had no choice!" Elke cried, interrupting Craig.

"You will remain silent, Miss Herrman!" Craig ordered. "Your involvement in this case is just as serious as Taylor's. In some ways, it's even more serious because you have been acting as a private personage, while Taylor at least had some official authority for part of his activities."

Craig glared at Elke until she lowered her eyes. Then he turned back to Mike, and addressed him. "Now, I'll grant you that the circumstantial material you've turned up is very interesting. But it does not justify your actions!"

"My actions are justified if I uncover a war criminal, and if I end his blackmailing of a person who was an original victim of his war crimes at Dachau," Mike countered. "How much more justification does there have to be?" he demanded angrily.

"Taylor, I can understand your feelings," Craig said sternly, yet with a certain amount of compassion. "The things that happened to your wife, and all that. But damn it! You know about the sensitive political implications that are involved. The very factors that made us conduct this investigation in such an odd way. And then, there was Kaufman's own request that it be called off. And State was very happy to do so!"

Craig shook his head. "And since then, everyone's been going along on the assumption that the whole thing had ended. And that any arms deal with Germany might, just might be possible at some future date. So what happens? You come in here with this…this story of yours. And you've got dead bodies in Paris and Rome. And now there'll have to be four governments involved, instead of just the U.S. and Germany."

"But I'm so completely certain!" Mike responded. "I'll bet anything on what we've got here. On the fact that Otto Behrens is Captain Max Schmidt. And that the bastard is not only a war criminal, but that he's still doing his dirty work. He's managed to intimidate Jacob Kaufman so badly, because of Kaufman's fear for his daughter's sanity, that Kaufman is paying blackmail to Schmidt, or Behrens, or whatever you want to call him. And I'm sure it's only going to get worse for Kaufman. He needs help. He needs help desperately!"

"And yet it was Kaufman who insisted that the investigation be called off," Craig pointed out. "Brought every pressure to bear, to do so, in fact!"

"Sure," Mike said. "Because his daughter had heard something. Right? And I'll bet it was Behrens who made sure the daughter *did* hear something. In order to force Kaufman to call things off. Look. The poor man managed to get up enough courage at one point to ask for the investigation. Probably because Behrens' demands were becoming excessive. But when I showed up in Europe, and Behrens discovered what I was up to, Kaufman's daughter was tipped off. Now, who the hell do you think did that? Behrens, of course! He was getting worried about the continuation of his blackmail money. That's obvious. And he knew that pressure on Kaufman's daughter would make Kaufman stop the investigation. And that's just what happened!"

"And so now, Kaufman is being tortured and robbed by Behrens, and we sit and do nothing!" Elke added unable to restrain herself, despite Craig's earlier warning.

After this outburst by Mike, and then Elke, Craig remained silent, thoughtful. Then he reached out and shuffled the various items Mike had laid before him on the desk. He looked at each carefully. Finally, he made up his mind.

"Okay, Taylor," he said to Mike, "I'm beginning to think there's a lot to your story. Enough, anyway, to justify my taking the matter up at State, or higher, if necessary. I'll fly down to Washington in the morning. But I want it in writing from you, first.

Just as you told it to me."

"Can do," Mike answered enthusiastically.

"But," Craig warned, "until I get some sort of reaction from State, I want you and Miss Herrman to stay put. No more investigating. No contacting Kaufman. No doing anything. Understand?"

"Yes," Mike answered.

"I'm warning you, Taylor. I mean this. This is still a very serious situation for you. Regardless of what you've turned up. Or what happens from this point on. Or what conclusions State draws. For one thing, there's that possible murder charge in Rome that will have to be straightened out. So I don't want you or Miss Herrman to do anything more. Now, is that understood?"

"Yes," Mike assured him.

"Miss Herrman." Craig turned to Elke. "I don't want to arrest you, officially. And I am assuming you will act in exactly the same manner as Mr. Taylor. Do you understand?"

"Yes sir."

"Okay," Craig concluded. "Now you get that report done," he told Mike, "while I set my appointments in Washington."

CHAPTER FORTY

Elke giggled, as she ran her hand over Mike's shoulders, across his chest and then down underneath the bed sheets.

"What's the giggling for?" Mike asked, shifting his body so that he could look into Elke's eyes as she lay beside him.

"Oh, I was thinking that obeying Craig's orders, about staying put and not doing anything, is really most enjoyable."

Mike grinned. "I don't really think Craig had quite this scene in mind, when he gave us those orders."

"Hardly," Elke agreed. She turned serious. "But it is most pleasurable, nonetheless." Then she smiled. "Do you think me forward, My Love, for admitting so freely how much I enjoy you in bed?"

Mike kissed her. "The only thing that I think you are, is wonderful."

"I am glad." Elke stretched her arms over her head and gave a satisfied sigh. "Oh, I feel so rested. What time is it?"

"Three thirty on a beautiful New York afternoon."

Elke shook her head. "It is only 24 hours since we met with Mr. Craig? So much has been happening."

"Uh huh. Only 24 hours."

"How do you feel?" Elke asked. "As rested as me?"

"Yes."

Elke laughed. "You know, it is so funny. For many years, I thought of visiting the United States, and especially New York. There were so many things I wanted to see. And now, I have been here for more than a day, and almost all I have seen is the ceiling of your bedroom."

"I'll admit it's not quite the same as the Statue of Liberty. Or the view from the Empire State Building. But we'll have plenty of time for those sights." Mike took Elke in his arms. "We have a lifetime for those sights."

Mike kissed Elke. Their kiss was interrupted by the ringing of the telephone. Reluctantly, they parted as Mike reached for the receiver.

"Hello?"

"Taylor, this is Craig."

"Yes sir," Mike responded, sitting up expectantly.

"Taylor, I'm in Washington now, and I'm talking from the State Department. I want you and Miss Herrman to be in my office tomorrow morning at 11:30 sharp."

"What's up? Did State agree to reopen the investigation?"

"No!" Craig responded strongly. "Emphatically, no. The decision's been made here at State not to reopen the investigation..."

"But why? I can't understand it. The evidence..."

"There's too much involved here, that's why. Listen! You're lucky you're not down here right now, being read out of the Service. State is furious with you for stirring up this thing again. And it took all I could do to keep them from throwing the book at you."

"What happens at 11:30 tomorrow morning?" Mike asked bitterly.

"Undersecretary Simmons is going to discuss with us how we can best get you out of that Rome killing jam. And also the problem about your having discovered the Rabbi's body in Paris. Now, you and Miss Herrman be there. And damn it, you better not give Simmons a hard time! Do you understand?"

"Yes, I understand," Mike answered grimly. "I understand completely."

Elke looked questioningly at Mike as he put down the receiver.

"State's decided not to reopen the investigation," he told her, the bitterness evident in his voice. "It's a political policy matter. And that's the end of that."

"Mike," Elke began quietly, soothingly. "I…I realize how hard it is to accept, but…"

"Goddamn political expediency!" Mike exploded. "Can't stir things up. Same goddamn political expediency everyone talked about in the 1930's. And look where the hell that got us. And now all over again. Goddamn political expediency! So Behrens goes free. And he keeps on blackmailing Kaufman. And

Kaufman keeps on paying. And the State Department is happy with its goddamn political expediency!"

"Mike! Please!" Elke cried. "Stop!"

The sharpness of Elke's voice forced Mike to look at her. For a moment, he stared, and then he took her hands in his. "I'm sorry, Elke," he said, his voice now more controlled. "It's just that I...I can't accept a decision like this."

"Perhaps at the meeting, tomorrow, you could try again, with this...this Undersecretary Simmons...?"

Mike shook his head. "Not a chance. By the time I see Simmons and Craig, the decision will be official past history. And nothing will change it." He thought for a moment. "That is, nothing will change it...except...except a renewed request from Jacob Kaufman to reopen the investigation!"

"But Kaufman is the one who asked that the investigation be stopped," Elke pointed out. "We know that."

"Yes, and we also know that he's frightened for his daughter," Mike said. "Now, if I could convince Kaufman that Behrens can be caught quickly and easily, without harm to his daughter, then I'll bet he'd agree to have the investigation reopened. I'll bet on it."

"You mean you still want to go to Jacob Kaufman?" Elke asked with alarm.

"That's one of the reasons we came to New York, isn't it?"

"But you cannot go to Kaufman," Elke protested. "Mr. Craig would be furious. It will...will ruin you! Your career! Your future!"

"No, Elke!" Mike answered strongly. "I can't accept that as a reason!" I've got to do this. I couldn't live with myself otherwise. I don't care what happens, but I've got to see Kaufman."

Elke regarded him for a moment. "I'm coming with you," she said .

CHAPTER FORTY-ONE

Mike decided it would be best to call on Jacob Kaufman unannounced, because he wasn't at all sure Kaufman would want to see him, now that the investigation had been stopped. He also decided to make the call at Kaufman's home, rather than his office, sensing that he would be able to talk more freely with the man in a non-business setting.

He and Elke arrived at Kaufman's residence, a town house on East 64th Street, between Lexington and Park, at 7:00 that evening. After considerable hesitation, Kaufman's butler led them into the library, where he left them while he went to announce their unexpected visit.

A few minutes later, Jacob Kaufman came in, looking very flushed. Mike started to shake hands, but checked the impulse as he noted Kaufman's brusque manner. Kaufman was the first to speak.

"Mr. Taylor," he said, the anger obvious in his voice, "I hardly expected to see you again. I had been assured that this investigation had been ended." He looked suspiciously at Elke.

"And who is this?

"Please, Mr. Kaufman," Mike began in a conciliatory tone, "I don't blame you for being angry. But I urgently ask that you listen to what I have to say. I'm sure that after you do, you'll see that we can help you."

"Help me?" Kaufman repeated the words and reflected on them. "You are here to help me? Is that your purpose?"

"Yes."

Kaufman shook his head. "I don't see how you can help."

"Please, Mr. Kaufman," Mike said, "please let me explain."

Kaufman was silent, and then he nodded.

"Alright, what is it you have to tell me?'

Mike answered, "When I first met you, Mr. Kaufman, and this investigation started, I was under the impression that the problem was mainly one of your receiving threatening letters from a diehard ex-Nazi who had somehow singled you out from among all the Jewish survivors of the concentration camps."

"Quite so," Kaufman said quickly. "And at the time I was anxious to have this matter ended."

"Yes. I know. But that wasn't the entire matter, was it, Mr. Kaufman?"

Kaufman's hands tightly gripped the arms of his chair. "I do not know what you mean," he said warily.

"Yes you do," Mike countered. "Mr. Kaufman, I want to help you. So, you must trust me."

They stared at each other for a moment.

Then, Mike, seeing that Kaufman was not going to respond, continued. "Very well, then. I see I've got to make things clear, and show you how much I really do know. Then, perhaps we can move on," he paused. "Mr. Kaufman, we know that Otto Behrens has been blackmailing you, and…"

"No!" Kaufman interrupted him, almost shouting. "That is not true!"

"…And that he is in reality a Captain Max Schmidt who was stationed at Dachau at the same time as you. And that he is getting money from you, under threat of contacting your daughter and possibly upsetting her mental balance."

Kaufman looked sharply at Mike, and for an instant he seemed puzzled. "What…what is it you said? About…about Otto Behrens being…a…a Captain Max Schmidt? At Dachau? Is…is that what you think?"

"That's what we know!" Mike answered quickly.

"And…and you believe this…this Captain Schmidt is blackmailing me? At the threat of upsetting my daughter? And that I am paying him sums of money?"

"Please, Mr. Kaufman," Mike pleaded, "please let's stop playing games with each other. Haven't I demonstrated to you that I know everything? Look. We're here to help you now. To end Behrens' hold on you and your family. Don't you see? He's a Nazi war criminal. He can be arrested and tried on that charge, and convicted. We can prove his guilt. And then he won't be able to threaten you, or to harm your daughter's sanity."

While Mike was speaking with Jacob Kaufman, Elke was looking at a small writing desk that was situated near where Kaufman was sitting. Now, while Mike and Kaufman continued to talk, Elke wondered how to get near the desk. She wanted to take a closer look at the top of it.

Kaufman asked Mike a question. "Do you know where Behrens is?" he inquired anxiously. "Do you know where he is, so you can arrest him?"

Mike shook his head. "No. Not exactly. But that's why we're here. Because you can help us find him. If you'll ask the State Department to reopen the investigation, they'll do so. Right now, State doesn't want to do anything. But if you request it, urge it, then State will agree to reopen the investigation. And then an official, and widespread government search can be made for Behrens. And he can be captured and brought to trial as Captain Max Schmidt."

Kaufman stood up. "No!" he said strongly. "No! You are wrong in everything. There is no blackmail. And as for your story about a…a Captain Max Schmidt, I do not know where you have obtained your information, but I cannot believe it. No! I will not ask that the investigation be reopened. I will not risk my daughter's peace of mind. Nothing is worth that."

"But…" Mike started to protest, only to be interrupted by Elke.

"Mr. Kaufman is absolutely right, Mike," Elke said loudly, and standing up. Mike stared at her, unbelieving as she continued.

"We have been wrong to come here and bother you, Mr. Kaufman. You must forgive our boorishness."

Even Kaufman seemed surprised at Elke's comments. Then, suddenly, Elke seemed to lose her balance, and she staggered forward, quite close to Kaufman's chair.

"Oh," she cried, almost falling down.

Both Mike and Kaufman reached out to steady her.

"What's the matter, Elke?" Mike asked, alarmed.

Elke shook her head. "It is nothing," she answered, reaching into her handbag for a handkerchief and patting her forehead. "Just a momentary dizziness."

"Do you want some water?" Mike asked.

"No. I am fine," Elke said. "And we must leave now."

"Yes. You must go," Kaufman said firmly. "There is nothing else to discuss. Mr. Taylor. I must ask that you do not return here again. I am sure, in fact, that even this time, you have come without authorization. However, I am willing to overlook it, but only if you will not come again!"

"You're making a grave mistake, Mr. Kaufman," Mike said.

"No. It is you who are making the mistake," Kaufman answered.

"Mike, we must go!" Elke urged.

Mike looked at Elke, totally perplexed at her behavior.

Then he stared at Kaufman's grim face. He realized that nothing further could be accomplished during this visit. He was still determined to somehow reopen the investigation. But he was aware that now was not the time to push. He walked angrily from the room.

CHAPTER FORTY-TWO

With effort, Mike contained his anger until he and Elke were on the street and out of sight of Kaufman's town house.

"Now what the hell was that all about?" Mike demanded, grasping Elke tightly by the arm. "Why did you torpedo me like that?" Then his tone softened as he looked very closely into her face. "And Elke, what's the matter with you? Don't you feel well? You almost fainted in there. What's wrong?"

"Nothing is wrong, Mike," Elke answered with excitement. "I did not faint. I did that on purpose."

"On purpose? But why?"

"For this. I took it off of the writing desk in Kaufman's library, when I staggered against it and almost fainted. That is, when I *seemed* to faint."

Puzzled, Mike looked at what Elke had taken out of her handbag.

"Damn!" he said sharply as he took the small piece of stationery paper from Elke.

"Doesn't it look familiar?" she asked with excitement.

Mike held the light blue writing paper up in front of him in order to examine it more closely.

"It certainly does," he said slowly, noting the texture of the sheet and the design of the water-mark. "It certainly does."

CHAPTER FORTY-THREE

When Mike and Elke entered Craig's office at 11:30 the next morning, Craig and Undersecretary of State George Simmons were waiting. It was obvious to Mike that they had been discussing him, and he sensed that he was going to be dressed down heartily.

"Taylor, Miss Herrman," Craig greeted them curtly. "This is Secretary Simmons," he introduced the dark haired and urbane Undersecretary.

When everyone was seated, and Undersecretary Simmons had nodded a go-ahead, Craig began the meeting. "Taylor," he addressed Mike, "all yesterday in Washington, Secretary Simmons and I met with various persons at State, to figure a way out of this mess that you created. It is an awful mess, Taylor," Craig said pointedly.

"Yes sir," Mike felt it appropriate to respond.

"In any event," Craig continued, "and despite the good deal of harm that has been done, we feel it is still possible to rectify matters. And that's what we plan to do, by taking a number of steps. Step number one is this: the investigation remains closed.

Just as ordered previously. Is that perfectly clear?"

"It's clear, Sir. But it can't be possible," Mike answered emphatically. "The investigation just can't remain closed. Not now, with what Miss Herrman and I know about it."

"Do I read you right, Taylor?" Craig asked angrily. "Do you know what you're saying? What you're doing? I'll have you..."

"Mr. Craig." The commanding voice of Undersecretary of State Simmons cut Craig short, and at the same time, arrested all other activity in the room. Craig, Mike and Elke all turned toward the Undersecretary.

"If I may," Simmons began calmly, but with the authority clear in his voice, "is it my understanding, Mr. Taylor, that you still are in disagreement with the decision? That you still believe the investigation should be renewed?"

"Definitely, Mr. Secretary. In view of new information that Miss Herrman and I have discovered, since last night, I know this investigation has to be opened again!"

"What happened last night?" Simmons asked.

"It was when we went to see Jacob Kaufman..." Mike started to explain.

"It was when you did what?" Craig interrupted Mike. "I told you to keep to your apartment. Taylor, you disobeyed orders again!"

"Taylor, this is most serious!" Simmons said strongly, even his usually calm exterior exhibiting unmistakable signs of anger. "You had absolutely no authority to do that! None whatsoever!

Don't you realize that you are playing with international stakes?"

"Yes sir," Mike answered. "And I realize how important all of this is. And I think you'll see that what we've discovered adds to the importance. If I can only be given the opportunity of speaking, and explaining my actions."

For a moment, there was an undecided silence in the room. Then Simmons nodded. "Go ahead, Taylor. Let us hear all the grisly details."

Mike paused to gather his thoughts. Then he began. "What started everything going, was what happened right after our meeting last night with Kaufman. Not before it. Or during it." Mike held out a piece of blue stationery paper. "Thanks to Miss Herrman's sharp eyes and nimble fingers, we took this piece of paper out of Kaufman's library. From off of a writing desk." Mike turned to Craig. "Do you have the scrap of paper I gave you yesterday? The one with that note on it that we found in Zeitling's apartment in Rome?"

Wordlessly, Craig pushed the manila file folder across his desk to Mike. Opening the folder, Mike took out the scrap of paper and held it and the larger sheet of blue stationery paper up toward Simmons. "You see? They match. They're exactly the same kind of paper. Same color, grade, texture and watermark." He held up the larger sheet. "This piece came from Jacob Kaufman's home." He held up the other sheet. "And this one was found in Zeitling's apartment, with instructions on it, probably to Zeitling, to kill the American and the German. Same paper. In Kaufman's home and in

Zeitling's apartment."

Mike put down the two pieces of paper. "Mr. Secretary," he addressed Simmons, "This fact, coupled with many others, has led us to the very careful conclusion that the man we are looking for is not Otto Behrens. The man we are looking for is, Jacob Kaufman. The Nazi war criminal in hiding is not Otto Behrens. It is, Jacob Kaufman. In short, our Captain Max Schmidt of Dachau is not Otto Behrens. He is, Jacob Kaufman!"

"Taylor," Craig protested, "Just because two pieces of paper look alike, how can you possibly come to that conclusion?"

"They're not just two pieces of paper," Mike answered quickly. "This morning, I checked with the stationery department at Tiffany's. This paper is private stock of theirs. Specially made. So specially made, in fact, that it is for only one customer."

"And that customer is Jacob Kaufman?" Undersecretary Simmons interjected.

"And that customer is, Jacob Kaufman," Mike affirmed.

Simmons leaned toward Mike. "Mr. Taylor, this is very interesting. Not conclusive yet. But interesting. Please go on."

"Let me backtrack a bit, first. That is, back to last night, after we had left Kaufman and had examined the sheet of paper. At that time, we of course hadn't yet checked with Tiffany's. So, we didn't know it was Kaufman's private stock. And we just had a lot of thoughts, but nothing concrete."

Mike paused and drew out his note pad from the breast pocket of his jacket. Then he resumed speaking. "The same theoretical conclusion hit both Miss Herrman and I as we looked at that piece of paper. The conclusion was this. Whoever had written that note to Zeitling, was Zeitling's boss. And to us, that meant Captain Max Schmidt, since we were assuming Zeitling was still serving the same person he had served during the war. Now, we had been assuming that Behrens was Schmidt. But the fact that the stationery in Zeitling's apartment, and the stationery in Kaufman's home were the same, led us to the other, newer conclusion. The conclusion that Kaufman, and not Behrens, was Schmidt. We knew it was a wild thought. But we decided to carry it through and see where it led us."

Mike paused again, and consulted his note pad. "One place it led us, was back to this fact. One of the strongest links of identification we had about Captain Schmidt was a description of his personality by Hans Zeitling's mother. As you know, we saw her in Heidelburg. She said her son had written that he was an aide to a Captain Max Schmidt who, and here I quote Mrs. Zeitling, 'was cultured in the fine things. He reads many books…Hans said his Captain was an authority on art, on painting.'"

Mike closed his note pad. "When we were in Heidelburg, both Miss Herrman and I came to the same conclusion. The description was a perfect fit, we thought, for Otto Behrens. After all, he evidently had some culture. At least it would seem that way to an awed kid corporal from Heidelburg, like Zeitling.

And Behrens was definitely somewhat of an authority on art and painting."

"So you concluded then, that Behrens and Schmidt were one and the same," Simmons said.

"Exactly," Mike answered. "Because then, at that time, Behrens already was a suspect, as far as I was concerned. He had, to be specific about it, been pointed out to me as a suspect by none other than Jacob Kaufman!" Mike paused to give emphasis to his next statement. "Now think about this, please. It's a conclusion Miss Herrman and I came to last night." Mike leaned forward intensely. "That description that Zeitling's mother gave us of Captain Max Schmidt? It actually fits Kaufman even better than it does Behrens! Kaufman definitely is far more cultured than Behrens. And certainly, he is more of an authority on art and paintings!"

"It's becoming increasingly interesting," Simmons said encouragingly. "Please continue."

"Next, Miss Herrman and I decided to see if we could find any more inconsistencies in the various conclusions and judgments we had previously made during the investigation." Mike opened his note pad again. "And here's one of them that we came up with. At my first meeting with Kaufman, before I went to Europe, he told me that he hadn't seen Otto Behrens in five years. Then, when I was in Rome, I had a long conversation with the concierge at the Albergo Dante. That's the place where Behrens had been living.

"The concierge told me that one night, someone came along with Zeitling, to visit Behrens. He didn't get a good look at the man, but he saw enough to tell me this. And these are the concierge's words: 'It was obvious that he was rich. Yes, very rich. Ah, I know cloths, Signore. Once I used to be in a clothing store. And I know a fine suit when I see it. And an expensive hat. A very expensive, how do you call it, a homburg?'"

Mike shrugged. "It's not a complete description, certainly. But I think you'd have to agree that Kaufman dresses expensively. And I know he wears homburgs. I saw one in his office. So, if he did visit Behrens in Rome, then he was lying to me, in New York, when he told me he hadn't seen Behrens in five years!"

"That entire supposition is a little bit weak, I'm afraid, Taylor," Simmons said. "That particular point wouldn't hold up very long. Too many men dress expensively and wear homburgs, for you to definitely establish that Kaufman visited Behrens in Rome."

"True," Mike conceded. "Except that there's more to support my theory," he said. "I took the liberty of checking at Customs this morning. For a list of Americans incoming from Rome, during all of September."

Craig interrupted. "It was in September that the concierge says he saw this expensively dressed man come into the hotel with Zeitling? To see Behrens?"

"Yes," Mike answered. "He wasn't sure of the date, but he was sure it was in September."

Mike consulted his note pad. "Anyway, I learned from Customs that one Jacob Kaufman returned to New York, from Rome, aboard TWA Flight #723, on September 17th."

"Interesting," Simmons said thoughtfully.

Mike stood up and paced about. "And there are so many other things, Mr. Secretary. Every time Miss Herrman and I started reviewing our material, we kept turning up other inconsistencies and initial misjudgements. For instance, isn't it interesting how Kaufman put on the pressure to have the investigation stopped, just when we seemed to be getting near to finding out who Captain Schmidt was, thanks to that diary that Miss Herrman found? Isn't it just a little too coincidental that the pressure to stop the investigation was applied by Kaufman just then?"

"And at last night's meeting," Elke broke in, "both Mike and I have since decided, that it appeared that Kaufman seemed very nervous to see us. And then a strange thing happened. As soon as we started saying we were going to help him, that we wanted to capture Behrens -- in other words, when it became obvious to him that we were not the slightest bit suspicious of *him*_-- then he was no longer nervous."

"Yes," Mike picked up the conversation. "And going way back, it was Kaufman who suggested to me that Behrens might be a suspect. That was at our first meeting. Kaufman also asked me then, if I carried a gun. I think that Kaufman was intending to use me as an instrument to get rid of Behrens, because Behrens was blackmailing him. I'm not absolutely sure why, yet. But I imagine it was because, somehow, Behrens knew about Kaufman's past, and especially about his wartime duty at Dachau. And there's one more thing, too, that ties in with Dachau."

"What is that?" Simmons asked.

"During my first meeting with Kaufman, I happened to mention that my wife had been a prisoner at Dachau. Kaufman became extremely agitated about this. But then, he calmed down, as soon as I told him that my wife was dead. At the time, his attitude struck me as strange. But I didn't pay any mind to it, figuring the subject of Dachau was just an emotional horror trigger that had set him off. But now, I realize it may have been because he was afraid my wife might be able to identify him as Captain Max Schmidt."

Mike stopped his pacing in front of Craig's desk. He picked up the two pieces of blue stationery paper. "A lot of what I've said is conjecture and circumstantial. I know that, Mr. Secretary. But these two pieces of paper are not. They are fact. Both pieces are from the same stock. And that stock is a private one, maintained by Tiffany's for only one person. And that person is Jacob Kaufman. That is a fact!"

Mike looked down at the two pieces of paper, and read aloud the fragment of writing from the torn piece. "…and so you must get the diary, and just as important, you must certainly kill them, the American and the German. The threat to our safety is too great. Use whatever means you must. It is most important."

Mike looked across at Simmons. "I say, Mr. Secretary, that Jacob Kaufman wrote these instructions to Hans Zeitling, and that Jacob Kaufman is Captain Max Schmidt."

The room was silent after Mike finished talking. Everyone

looked at Undersecretary Simmons, who was concentrating on sifting and sorting what Mike had told him.

Finally, Simmons broke the silence. "It is difficult to dismiss what you have said, Mr. Taylor. Yes, it is conjecture. But it's damned persuasive conjecture. I must admit that much." He shook his head. "First Behrens is Schmidt. Then Kaufman is Schmidt. Fantastic. Utterly fantastic."

"Mr. Secretary," Mike said, "It's not only fantastic, but I think it's also true! And I feel strongly that there is enough here to question Kaufman. Right now!"

Simmons thought for a moment. "Since I cooperated with Mr. Kaufman when we first started this investigation," he reasoned aloud, "I can't see why he could object now, if I were to ask him a few questions." He rose. "Let's go," he ordered.

CHAPTER FORTY-FOUR

A short while later, after traveling uptown in a government limousine, Mike, Elke, Craig and Simmons arrived at Kaufman's office on 57th Street between Park and Madison.

The receptionist quickly rang inside, and shortly, Kaufman's secretary appeared. It was the same woman who had met Mike on his previous visit to the office. She gave Mike a slight nod of recognition as Simmons addressed her.

"Is Mr. Kaufman in? We want to see him," Simmons said.

The woman recognized authority when she saw and heard it. "No sir," she said respectfully. "He left a short while ago."

"And when will he return?" Simmons asked.

"Not today, I don't believe. He had to go up to the lodge. With an unexpected business visitor."

"The lodge?" Simmons asked.

"Yes sir," the secretary answered. "Mr. Kaufman has a lodge in Armonk, New York. For meetings. He often takes business associates there. So he won't be disturbed. There is no telephone on the premises."

Mike had a sudden, wild hunch, and he addressed Kaufman's secretary. "Did you say this business visitor was unexpected?"

"Yes."

"Do you know his name?" Mike asked.

For an instant, the secretary hesitated.

"His name?" Simmons insisted.

The secretary shook her head. "I don't know it, Sir. Mr. Kaufman usually tells me these things. But in this case, he never did let me know the gentleman's name."

"What did he look like?" Mike asked, still pursuing his hunch.

The woman thought for a moment. "Well, I didn't get that good a look at him. He was here only a short time. And as I say, he wasn't expected. He wasn't on Mr. Kaufman's list of appointments. And in fact, even Mr. Kaufman seemed surprised to see him."

"What did he look like?" Mike persisted.

"Well, he had one distinctive feature that I couldn't forget. It was his nose. It was kind of…kind of bent to the left side of his face, and…"

"And he was about 5 feet 9 inches tall, weighed about 155 or 165 pounds, and had very thin hair which was dirty brown and streaked with gray. Right?" Mike finished the description for her.

"How did you know?" the secretary asked in surprise.

"It's Behrens!" Mike said to Simmons, disregarding the secretary's inquiry. "I bet it's Behrens. The description fits perfectly!"

"Behrens? Here in New York?" Simmons asked

"Why not?" Mike thought aloud. "It makes a lot of sense. After what happened in Rome, Behrens knew he was in trouble. And that he would have to hide out. So, maybe he decided to hit Kaufman for a final bundle of money. A big lump sum. And what better way to collect, than to come here himself."

Simmons looked at Craig. "How quickly could you find out from Customs if Behrens entered the country within the last two days?"

"In about 15 minutes," Craig answered.

"Mr. Secretary," Mike addressed Simmons, "If it is Behrens who is with Kaufman, and I'm almost sure it is, then I suggest we follow them up to the lodge. If we can catch them together, we may be able to break the case wide open. Confronted together like that, one or the other of them might crack."

"Good idea," Simmons agreed. He turned to Craig. "Call Customs for the information on Behrens," he told him. "And have them call us back on the limousine telephone." Then he spoke to Kaufman's secretary. "I want directions on how to reach Mr. Kaufman's lodge," he ordered.

CHAPTER FORTY-FIVE

The drive to the lodge at Armonk, in upper Westchester, took slightly over an hour. About half way up, the telephone call came from Customs, reporting that Behrens had entered New York at 7:00 that morning.

With their suspicions confirmed, Simmons, Craig and Mike discussed how best to confront Kaufman and Behrens. Kaufman's secretary had told them that the lodge was in a secluded area, off Route 22, near the Hutchinson River Parkway and that it was reached by a narrow service road. Mike suggested that they leave the car near the base of the service road, and approach the house on foot, going through the heavy woods that Kaufman's secretary told them surrounded the building. The element of surprise, he stressed to Craig and Simmons, was probably their best tactic.

"If we can just surprise them together," Mike said, "And especially with you present, Mr. Secretary, I'm sure one of them will start talking."

The lodge, Kaufman's secretary also had told them, was about three quarters of a mile up the service road.

And now, as the limousine turned off Route 22 and onto the service road, Simmons ordered the driver to stop.

Simmons turned to Elke. "Miss Herrman," he told her. "You had better remain here, with the driver."

"Please, Sir," Elke pleaded, "I want to come along. I have been so much involved in this, I must be allowed to come."

Simmons nodded. "All right. But stay in the rear, please."

With Mike in the lead, the group left the car and began walking up the service road toward the lodge. After a short walk, the road curved slightly to the right, and at this point, Mike turned and moved into the dense woods. Followed by Craig, Simmons and Elke, in that order, he picked his way through the trees until he saw the lodge, in a clearing, about 25 yards in front of them.

Mike stopped and motioned the others to join him. "It looks like we're in luck, he said, pointing at the lodge. "That seems to be the back of the building, so we should be able to get up close without being seen. I'd suggest that we split up, though. I can cut around the woods and come in toward the front of the house, while you enter from the rear. Then…"

"Look!" Elke interrupted. "The door is opening!"

They turned to look at the lodge, just as a door swung open, and Behrens came out.

"I'll be damned," Mike whispered, as Behrens stepped forward, his arms raised above his head. And following a short distance behind Behrens, Kaufman came out holding a hand gun.

Mike reached for his own gun, as Behrens and Kaufman

walked slowly across the clearing, directly toward them.

"He's going to kill him!" Mike said urgently, starting to move forward. "We've got to stop Kaufman!"

But it was too late. Mike had gone only a few yards, when Kaufman raised his gun, aimed at Behrens' back, and fired from a distance of a few feet.

Behrens pitched forward, and Kaufman fired a second shot into his neck.

Mike ran into the clearing. "Kaufman!" he shouted.

Kaufman whirled toward Mike.

"Drop your gun!" Mike ordered.

Kaufman hesitated, but then he started to raise his weapon in Mike's direction. Seeing the movement, Mike dropped to one knee, aimed, and squeezed the trigger. At the short distance of no more than 5 yards, the shot rang true, and the bullet ripped into Kaufman's chest. Mike started to fire a second time, but didn't, as Kaufman fell to the ground.

Mike and the others ran to the two bodies. Behrens was motionless, but Kaufman was still alive. Mike bent down, as Kaufman tried to speak.

"I should have known! I should have realized you knew more than you seemed to!" Kaufman heaved the words out at Mike between labored breaths.

"Schmidt. Captain Max Schmidt of Dachau," Mike addressed Kaufman. "Right?"

"Yes," Kaufman admitted.

"And Behrens was blackmailing you. He knew your true identity."

Kaufman nodded. "Is he dead?"

"Yes."

"I am glad," Kaufman said. He laughed weakly, and with bitterness. "It was perfect. Until he found out. For 20 years, it was perfect."

Kaufman coughed. Blood began to trickle from the corner of his mouth. He fought to catch his breath, and then his body sagged into death.

CHAPTER FORTY-SIX

"Have you finished examining the letters?" Craig asked Mike. It was two days later, in Craig's office, and Mike and Elke were meeting with him.

"Yes, and they explain almost everything," Mike answered. "Right down to the last detail."

He laid the sheaf of letters on Craig's desk. The letters had been found in Kaufman's apartment. They were letters between Kaufman and Behrens, and between Kaufman and Zeitling.

"Give me a summary of what's in there," Craig ordered.

"The main thing they show," Mike began, "Is that Behrens just had blind luck in pinpointing Kaufman as being the ex-Nazi Captain Max Schmidt. It seems that Behrens was a sergeant in that Munich General Headquarters records department. His real name was Bruno Mueller. And he was in charge of all official German Army personnel records that were forwarded from Dachau. As a result of this, he was familiar with Captain Max Schmidt's record and identity."

"But when did the blackmail start?" Craig asked.

"Certainly not right after the war?"

"No," Mike answered. "Behrens didn't even run into Kaufman until about six months ago. In Rome. That was the first time he saw him, since the end of the war. And it was shortly after that, that he started blackmailing him."

Craig shook his head. "And yet, when you first met with him, Kaufman told you that he had business dealings with Otto Behrens, about five years before."

"Just part of his cover story, I imagine," Mike said. "Hell, that entire meeting I had with him, must have been phony, in retrospect."

"You mean all of the details he gave you?" Craig asked.

"Yes. He was just setting me up. Behrens must have started getting too exorbitant in his money demands, and Kaufman figured it was time to get rid of him. And he hoped to use the United States government to do so."

"But why bring the government into it?" Elke asked.

Mike shrugged. "Some sort of a devious, roundabout plot of his. I'm not really sure exactly what he had in mind. But I am sure he never expected that diary of his to turn up. I'm sure he thought it was destroyed long ago. But when it turned up, that must have been the point when he started panicking, and applying pressure to have the investigation called off."

"How about those letters Kaufman showed the State Department?" Craig asked. "How do those fit in?"

"That's all explained in Kaufman's letters of instruction to

Zeitling," Mike answered. "It seems those blackmail letters that Kaufman showed State were part of his plotting. He had Zeitling type them up himself, at each of the hotels where Behrens used to stay. In other words, he was setting up a frame of Behrens, with those letters."

"And that explains about that phrase that tipped you off," Craig said. "The phrase that appeared both in the diary and in the letters. What was it again? About being a good German, and the duty of killing Jews? Or something like that?"

"Right," Mike confirmed. "As devious as he was, Kaufman tripped himself up with that one. I bet he didn't even realize he was using that phrase in each of the four blackmail letters. And that he had used that same phrase, over 20 years before, in his Dachau diary."

Craig picked up a sheet of paper from his desk. "And this bank report just about cleans up the last detail," he said, passing the paper over for Mike's examination.

Mike glanced at it. "The dates come pretty close, don't they. Every time Kaufman drew a personal check for cash, a few days later, Behrens deposited approximately the same amount in his bank in Rome."

"An epitaph of records," Elke interjected.

Both Mike and Craig looked at her

"What did you say?" Mike asked.

"I was remembering something Behrens said," Elke replied. "About the mania that Germans have for keeping records." She nodded her head toward the pile on the desk, which was composed of the diary, the sheaf of letters and the bank report.

"He was so damned meticulous about keeping records," Mike said. "Records were Kaufman's epitaph, all right. And they were something else, too."

"What's that?" Craig asked.

"His downfall," Mike told him.

THE END

SAUL WARSHAW

Also by Saul Warshaw
WILL JONAS MYSTERY SERIES
Killing Memories
A Killing Business
Bang Bang You Are Dead
Manifesto
You Remember You Die
Loose Ends
Mind Tricks

Want to read another book by Saul Warshaw? Why not try his latest Will Jonas, Private Investigator mystery novel? It's called LOOSE ENDS/MIND TRICKS. And it is available as an e-book on Kindle or in a print edition from Amazon.

Excerpt for Loose Ends

CHAPTER 1

THE YEAR 2004

Rose Shapiro, my secretary-receptionist-bookkeeper-Jewish mother-everything called on the intercom.

"A Mr. Martin Gershon is on the line. He says he is a lawyer, and he needs to talk to you."

The "you" in this case – is me.

I'm Will Jonas, and for the last nine years, I've been running a private investigations agency, which I started after I retired from the Los Angeles Police Department, where I'd put in 30 years, most of them as a homicide detective.

I didn't recognize Gershon's name – but when a lawyer calls, it's usually because he has some investigative work for me to do.

So of course, I picked up my phone. Hey, I always can use new clients.

"Mr. Gershon," I said, "What can I do for you?"

"Mr. Jonas, you can listen to what I have to say – and then I hope you'll agree to go with me to the State prison in Lancaster, to talk with my client."

"Whoa, let me interrupt you right there. I have to tell you that if I had a nickel for every inmate who sends me letters claiming his innocence – if only I could help – well, I'd be retired and working on my golf game."

"This is different," Gershon came back at me. "My client is not the subject here. It's his cellmate. My client believes the guy has been railroaded into prison for up to 11 years, for a crime he did not commit. Even though he did plead guilty. But my client says there are – what he calls 'very odd circumstances' that make the whole conviction suspect."

"Look, Mr. Gershon…"

"Call me Marty."

"Okay, Marty. What you're telling me *is* a little different, since it's not your client who's claiming he was wrongly convicted. I see that. But what makes your client capable of deciding that his cellmate is innocent? Is your client one of those jailhouse lawyer types?"

"No, he's not. Let me explain. First off, my client is now a third of a way through a 20-year sentence for murder. That charge is not going to change, and his sentence is not going to be reduced. In other words, he's not getting any sort of a deal here.

"But before he was convicted, my client had a doctorate in psychology, and a successful practice. And since he's been in prison, he's kept at it. Informally, of course. And over the years, he's helped many prisoners deal with their rougher mental health problems.

"And what he's telling me is that this cellmate of his—and he's only been his cellmate for several weeks – is not guilty. He is convinced that the man did not commit the murder for which he's been convicted."

"Still, Marty," I came back at Gershon, "What you're telling me is a lot of subjective stuff. Nothing factual. And I just don't see how I can help."

"Will, when my friend in prison asked me to help, I knew I'd need a top flight investigator with a background in homicide. I did a computer search. Saw your name, among others. And then I Googled you. Interesting stuff. You and your partner, Charlie Black, solved a lot of high visibility homicides. Got a lot of press coverage.

"And as I read through those clippings, there was something you said, that convinced me you were the investigator I wanted.

"You were talking about the need to make sure policing and justice were not just for the privileged. They were for everyone. And sometimes, in order to bring justice to the underprivileged, you and your partner would bend the rule book.

"Will, do you remember saying that?"

"Yes...but..."

"No 'buts' Will. You said it. And here's an opportunity for you to live up to what you said. You'll be compensated for your work of course. My firm will put you on retainer, as soon as you agree. Come on, Will. Let's bring some justice to someone who just might be innocent."

Marty went silent. Like any good lawyer, he knew when to end his argument – his summation – on a high note.

"Okay, Marty," I gave in. "You win."

ABOUT THE AUTHOR

After careers as a broadcast journalist and then a public relations counselor, Saul Warshaw, at age 87, is now happily enjoying his third career as a writer. Five of his novels have been published. Saul and his wife Vivian, both ex-New Yorkers, are longtime residents of Los Angeles. If you would like to write Saul, please do so at:

Saul1warshaw@gmail.com

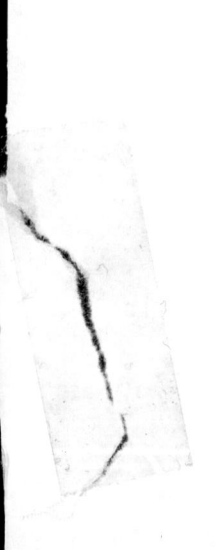